THE *Ghosts* OF PAW PAW LAKE

MARK SIMONE

Illustrations by Dan Simone

SABELO PRESS

The Ghosts of Paw Paw Lake
All Rights Reserved.
Copyright © 2015 Mark Simone
v2.0

Cover Photo © 2015 thinkstockphotos.com.
Author Photo by Marty Culbertson.
Illustrations by Dan Simone
All rights reserved - used with permission.

Sabelo Press
www.ghostsofpawpaw.com

ISBN: 978-0-578-16259-1

PRINTED IN THE UNITED STATES OF AMERICA

Dedication

This book is dedicated to the memories of my wonderful parents who have left us for their places in the Heavens.

Samuel Simone

Hebert Floyd

Becky Gladish

Contents

Acknowledgement

The Top Honors acknowledgements for this work of fiction go to a worker of hard reality, Eric Wrisley. My pal Eric not only edited it, but edited these pages many times. I don't know what kind of writer I may be or may become, but any sense of polish or success with these stories is genuinely due to Eric's loving counsel, teaching and careful reading. Holding a Master's Degree in Professional Writing and Editing, I do not exaggerate when I say that I am glad he spent all that money on college so I could be a beneficiary!

So this book is dedicated to you, Sir Wrisley. Thank you so much for being a great friend and a wonderful reader, critic and editor. You are one class act!

I also want to thank my oldest son, Daniel, for his beautiful, clever illustrations for this book. It was inspiring to watch your imagination reflect what I was seeing in my mind as it would unfold and appear on your drawing pad. I love it that you insisted on perfection, even if I missed my self-inflicted "due dates" for getting this in to the publisher. I am so proud that we could collaborate in the truest sense of "Ice Ice Baby".

Finally, thanks to my wife, Kathy, who has read these stories for years and served as proofreader and clarifier of confusing passages. I remember her honest encouragement after reading my first couple of stories all those years ago. She told me that she was glad they were good, because what if they weren't? How do you tell an aspiring hubby to take up painting?

Chagrin Falls, Ohio
January 1 2015

Disclaimer

The only constant in this book that is real is that I do live on Paw Paw Lake in South Russell, Ohio, just four miles east of Chagrin Falls, which is also a real place. The people and places, while occasionally named after someone I know or in places I have shopped or visited, are not in any sense real. It's all how my imagination pictured it. And, as far as I know, the ghosts are also fictitious.

Foreword

> "Probably every fourth person you talk to has had
> an experience with a poltergeist or ghost – or knows
> someone who has."

> Steven Spielberg, 1982

I did not always believe in ghosts. I came to that belief on my own through some pretty incredible realizations that I experienced with some of my family members. We definitely agree with the statistic that maintains some 15% of our population*, although rational and not looking for ghosts, believe that they have encountered ghosts in one fashion or another. Inexplicable and incredible as the experience may have been, they admit it can only be explained by something outside of the realm of our physical understanding.

However, if this book were intended to take up this argument of ghosts, and attempt to convince you as reader that you are surrounded by ghosties and specters, then it will be a failure. This is not an apologetic for the supernatural. Rather, it is simply stories for the sake of having fun dreaming them up and telling them.

This project began in the early '90's on a January 2nd when I decided I had some interesting rumblings flying around in my cranium. I started writing down some of what I called my "strange stories", none of which are in this collection. Over time, the stories became the ghost stories you have here. This collection represents about a third of the stories I wrote in that year or two of imagining what it would be like to live with ghosts. And of great interest to me now, as I wrote these stories while listening to Midnight Oil, The B-52's, Weezer, Pearl Jam and some Nirvana in rotation with The Beatles, Stones and The Allman

Brothers, is that they still stand up with Locksley, The Dollyrots, The Black Keys and Jack White. In the 90's I was still ghost-skeptical. I would not have my first personal "ghost event" until 1999, and again in 2004. Real chillers they were and they required that I reconsider my spectral cosmology. Those encounters have made me believe in hindsight that these stories could perhaps have happened someplace and in some real time.

So here are my stories. I hope you get a bit of a chill and I hope you like them.

Blessings and Peace –
MAS
May 2015

*These findings are offered by Professor Ian Stevenson of the University of Virginia in Charlottesville and presented in the book *True Hauntings* edited by Peter Haining, 2008, Konecky and Konecky.

A Reverend's Regret

Drawing deeply on a hand carved pipe he picked up near an ashram in India, Reverend Alexander Sinclair reviewed his Sunday sermon notes once again. It was to be delivered on the morrow at all three services and it needed to be exact and perfect. He hoped and prayed that it would curb the madness of unbridled imagination that was currently plaguing the Chagrin Valley and the communities therein.

"Positive proof" was being offered at nearly every breakfast gathering numbering more than one diner. The same was being advanced in the discussions along the grocery store aisles, the hair salons, as gas was being pumped, and among casual "cone lickers" as they gathered for ice cream in the Chagrin Falls version of a town square, the Triangle. It was not good and Rev. Sinclair could no longer ignore the communal unknowingness of such important spiritual material. To overlook the power of the spoken myth or fable would be to encourage the interest in beliefs commonly linked to the minions of Hell.

While not a pastor to be overly concerned by the primitive usage of Satan's presence as a tool of intimidation used by parents wanting their children to pick up their toys or go to sleep, he was not comfortable in allowing these beliefs to permeate daily civil intercourse among adults. To use the devil as a surrogate paddle for gaining obedience was bad parenting. To not stand firmly against seeing a spirit under every rock was irresponsible pastoral leadership. So, let the masses beware on the Lord's Day. Reverend Alexander Sinclair was going to give them a real dose of Hell.

Relighting his pipe, Sinclair looked again over the top edge of his finished manuscript and gazed at the light of the setting sun as it washed and rippled among the gentle waves of Paw Paw Lake. His deck held the lake in perfect view, framing it as if seen through the eye of a careful and skilled painter rendering it on canvas. He could not resist the interplay of nature and humanity, precisely and painstakingly blended in the perfect balance of the natural and the rustic. These delightful homes, his being one, were not simply built into nature as some ghastly intrusion. Rather, they were almost tucked into the surroundings, as a mother nestles her first born into her warm and comfortable crib following nursing. His home was, in many ways, a womb within the splendors of the undisturbed landscape.

Setting down his pipe and sheaf of papers, he rose and walked down the steps of the deck toward the lake. A casual breeze ruffled his hair. His untucked shirt billowed out like a sail. He felt so free, so sure of his mission, so in touch with the cosmic unifying factor of all of life. Of course, as a Presbyterian minister holding a Doctorate of Theology, he knew this force as God, the Almighty. But to accept the notions of the divine as understood in other world faiths seemed proper. Sort of an amalgamation of all religious sentiment suited him fine.

His momentary abandonment was interrupted by the passing of Mrs. Weatherhead and her sister, Mrs. Fabian of Dubois, Pennsylvania. Both were Catholics who had not attended Mass in years, except for the pilgrimages of Easter and Christmas. Both were about as annoying as a turtle might be if caught in one's throat. As they passed him in their circling sojourn along the lake's walking path, they returned to their conversation. Mrs. Weatherhead was deep in her commitment to bring her sister up to date on the rash of alleged sightings. The very sightings he would undertake in his services tomorrow.

"It's true, Angela," continued Mrs. Weatherhead, "so many people have seen the ghosts that I can't but believe them. The spirits are among us."

"I hope I never see one." said a frightfully agitated Mrs. Fabian.

Calling over his shoulder, Rev. Sinclair could not resist interjecting, "You'll never see what does not exist, ladies." He broke an expansive grin as one remarked a mumbled, "Well I never…"

As he tidied his evening dishes, Rev. Sinclair scanned the letter from his sister, Tillie, which reached him from Paris only this morning. With bits of suds on his hands, he turned page two to page three, leaving a generous dab of bubbles on the edge of the sheet. As she told of her children growing and experiencing the trials and joys of life, he felt the slight pang of regret that seemed to hit him at night, of not taking a wife and raising a family of his own. He was not a generous man, nor one of patience. Sharing his life with a woman and children of his own would have been a great difficulty. Yet, reading of Thomas and Amelia, Tillie and Roger's twins, he wondered what it might have been like to be a father, husband, even a better brother. This was Tillie's third letter since he last wrote her. Sighing in regret for both omissions, he dried his hands and reviewed his sermon a last time.

"For the God of love who empowers us to follow the truth would not send us the stumbling of intentional fiction met with human fancy. We are God's Ambassadors to bring truth to this planet, not stories founded in bored minds unable to grasp the changing culture of modern living and progress. For history shows us that the forward motion of the strong is always delayed by the witless prattling of the cowardly, which would have us restore the darkness to our illuminated lives through tales of supernatural visitations. Be sure, good people, that God in his majesty and might will not tolerate these erosive stories of ghosts and night visions, sent to seed our minds with the fearful in the name of the unknown, and neither will I."

He could hear the whispers of drama as his truth descended upon the ears of the hungry. It would be a moving sermon and likely receive some repeating of its own in the grocery, the salon, and the sidewalk. Putting the sermon in his briefcase, he retired to his room for the night's rest promised to the righteous.

The next morning as he shook the hands of his parishioners

following the third service, he was gratified to note that his efforts of controlling the hysteria in the community were bountifully returning a crop of confirming agreements. No trite comments of "nice sermon, pastor" this morning. Instead, he was greeted by words of concurring and accord made only better when the ancient Mr. Swarts leaned over, intending to whisper (he was nearly stone deaf) and spoke a resounding "Give 'em hell, pastor. What else can you say if they ain't got the brains to see through the crap." Rev. Sinclair chuckled as he relived that moment over and over again. Turning into his driveway, he decided to note "Swartie's" little remark in his journal.

Pulling over to his mailbox, Rev. Sinclair retrieved his morning paper from the blue paper box next to his mailbox. Where Sunday morning was committed to the delivering of the Word of God, Sunday afternoon was given to silent consideration of each and every news page in the thick tube of paper he pulled into his car. Undoing the rubber band, he perused the headlines noting that war was being considered in two parts of the world, another jet crashed killing 137, the temperatures would rise yet again this week, and next week would find our president on a nine day tour of eastern Europe and Japan. As he slid his toe off of the brake to coast to his driveway, he let his eye wander to the baseball scores above the masthead to see how well the Indians had trounced Toronto. An enormous slam on his car hood brought him up in his seat, his foot crushing the brake.

In front of him, hands still on the car, his eyes met the most delicate shade of blue he had ever seen set deftly in the sockets of the most beautiful woman he had ever gazed upon. She had red hair, freckles, a determined forehead, and appeared to stand tall and slim when fully erect.

"This may be your home but it certainly is not your road." She said in a rising voice.

Putting his car in park and opening the door he said, "I don't understand. What do you mean?" Instantly he thought of a number of better responses.

"I said," She repeated, "It's your house, but we all are permitted the use of the road. Running me down is in direct violation of my right to walk on the road. You were about to run me over."

"Madame, I assure you, I had no such intention. Running you over was not on my list of scheduled activities this day." He felt like his more collected self now that the words were again at his command. *I wonder how old she is.*

"Intention or not, you nearly showed me the underside of this gas guzzling land yacht as you passed over my writhing carcass. Not where I planned spending my Sunday."

Shaken, Rev. Sinclair realized that this was not a battle worth defending. Her description of being run over by his car outweighed his need to be right. He had not seen her in front of him and, as a result, might have killed her.

"I apologize with every possible regret, Madame. I have no excuse. I did not see you. Had you not slapped the hood I may well have run you down and would never have found the grace to forgive myself." He could feel his face redden and his heart began to beat terribly fast. *I almost killed this marvelous creature. Wonder where she lives?*

She pushed off from his car and straightened her blue gingham summer dress. Absently, she smoothed her hair and walked to his side of the car, keeping the door between them. She extended her hand.

"I'm Marilyn Morgan," she said waiting for his hand to lift above the door for a shake. "I'm sorry I snapped at you and I accept your apology."

I get to touch her, he thought as he took her hand. "I am truly sorry. I was browsing the headlines and neglected to look any farther. I don't quite know what to say."

"Nice to meet you often fits a handshake. Apology accepted. No damages. And I don't even feel compelled to instruct you to be more careful next time. See you around." And she began a marked stride away, up the road toward the woods which circled Paw Paw Lake.

"Goodbye…" he said as he watched her trek away. As she resumed her walk into the woods, she flipped a hand over her head in a wave but did not look back. When she was absorbed by the forest, he climbed back into his car. His favorite neighbor, JJ Gadd, gave his patented double horn toot and leaned out of his window to yell his characteristic greeting, "Hey Rev. How's the saving going?" Always the same with JJ. Rev. Sinclair smiled back and pulled into his driveway, lowering the garage door automatically before leaving the car. Before entering his house, he looked through the garage door windows again to the place in the woods she entered. He saw nothing.

After a microwaved lunch, through which he simultaneously consumed a good quarter of the week's news, he moved his lemonade and paper to the back porch. The sun was warm and relaxing as it heated his body to the point of a fine sweat. From the kitchen he could hear the phone machine come on and listened with satisfaction as Nicholas Marks, one of the church deacons, praised him for his timely sermon. Mentally he tallied again, adding Nick's call to the 16 already covering the tape. *Hit the nail on the head,* He thought as he opened the travel section.

It was late afternoon, the sun already dipping behind the trees on his property, when he awoke from his nap. The paper had fallen to the deck and his neck hurt slightly from the odd angle of the Adirondack chair. It was a great chair to sit and watch the world over his back deck rail, but nearly debilitating when used for naps. The design of the chair made it so that his neck was pushed forward a bit too much.

Turning his neck to loosen it, he noticed a blue flash in the woods where the sun was still sinking. It was that gingham woman, still walking by the lake. At least, he thought it must be her. The blue seemed the same as what she was wearing. He rose and went to the railing but could see no other signs of her. *Pity. I'd love to see her again.* Picking up the papers, he went in for the Indians game just beginning in Seattle.

The final score was Indians - 6, Mariners - 2. Before bed, he noted that the final phone message tally was 27, all supporting his discourse against the fables of the community. Sometimes all the chips come your way.

In Tuesday's mail, an anonymous letter called him a "cynic whose unbelief colors your understanding." Two phone messages, also anonymous, characterized him as a "scientific jerk" and a "blind reprobate." Now there was a Bible word not often used. Honesty demanded that he list his sermon score as 27 - 3.

It wasn't until Wednesday that he saw the woman in blue gingham again. She had come to his mind a few times and was, in fact, the focus of his thoughts as he set out from his back deck to seek the solitude of the lake. Deciding to walk the community footpath, he saw her plainly on the other side of the lake, walking at an intentional pace. Thinking she was looking, he waved. If she saw him, she did not acknowledge it. He felt sad that she was so distant. He would have shouted a greeting had she turned.

And so it went that Rev. Sinclair, champion of the modern enemies of fables, sought to bring rational thinking to the Chagrin Valley. The local paper carried his sermon, in excerpts and with his permission, which allowed his logical presentation of spiritual matters to spread further throughout the lake communities and the rest of the valley itself. The barrage of ghost sightings and stories, which had become almost epidemic, was now replaced by consideration of his missive. It was gratifying to hear the phone ring for it brought continued confirmation that he was making a difference in his world. He was debunking those who had no depth of character, feeling perfectly justified in telling tales of apparitions. The dead returning to visit. Promises of the sick being made well. Ghosts that protected, brought justice, or revealed the hidden to the living. It was all rather primitive and childish. In fact, it was deplorable. *I wonder what effect this community wide discourse will have on our attendance.* He was certain that God would bring an increase.

Seemingly, but certainly not likely, as his sermon spread to the populous, his sightings of the blue clad woman also rose. She seemed to be everywhere, but that was improbable. He might catch a peripheral glimpse of her as he entered the small community of Paw Paw Lake, standing just beyond the shrubbery. In his rear view mirror, he might see her pass on the road as he parked his car. Making coffee, he thought he noted her up near his mailbox. However, each time he positioned himself to look with full attention, it seemed she passed from his sight. *I'd just love to talk to her again.*

His chance came later, just as the fervor of his now famous sermon was declining in the Valley. She was again just there. Not as an appearance, like the ghosts he had so effectively "chased" from the valley through his illustrative words; words that had obviously illuminated the general public. No, her coming was one of turning to find himself face-to-face with her as he pivoted to return home from a walk.

Her hand was raised as if she was just about to tap him on the shoulder. Her mouth slightly open as if to say something to bring his attention to her. They looked at each other and, suddenly, as the startled faces cleared, both began to laugh.

His mother had always believed that laughter was the "mindless expression of those too unaware or uncivilized to enjoy the fullness of an expressive smile." His father, in disagreement, had believed that laughter was "the quickening of the mind in glorious agreement with God's provision to cleanse the soul of the somber thinking that we might be free of gloom." Rev. Sinclair had always favored his mother's opinion over his father's until that moment of laughing with the woman in blue gingham.

"Oh, you startled me so." He said between bursts of tittering.

"It's a payback for trying to run me over." She returned.

"Fair is fair." He agreed. They stopped their receding giggles as their eyes clasped in unwavering connection.

Breaking the stare, the woman turned with him and began

walking back with him. He hesitated only the distance of a stride and joined her.

"You are the Rev. Sinclair who has responded to the stories in the community about the presence of ghosts." She began.

"Yes, I am he."

"So, it would not be unfair to say that you are an unbeliever."

"If by that you mean that I do not believe in the supernatural realm of the spiritual capacity of all humanity, you would be in error. However, if your comment is based on the belief that we have suddenly been overtaken by the spirits of the dead as they haunt us, or at least try to communicate with us, then you would not be far from my position."

Slowing, she looked at his face; he resisted looking back by carefully surveying the black topped road in front of him as they emerged from the wooded path.

"Who teaches people to talk like that, anyhow? What would be wrong with saying, 'I don't buy the ghost stories' instead of that mouth full? I have to decipher what I think you may have said which leaves me little time to hold an intelligent conversation."

Anger flared in Rev. Sinclair's heart like a sun spot. Numerous rebuttals fought for the right to be spoken, but only an apology slipped out.

"I guess it's just habit. In seminary, we tend to write like that. After a time it becomes our manner of professional speech. I don't know why I talk like that." He did not feel embarrassed saying this, as he thought he might.

"Now, that I understand. Anyway, why don't you believe in ghosts?" she asked.

"What's to believe? It is the extension of all of our fears. That we just die with no second chance or eternal record. We hate to think that this is it, so we create the ghosts who bring us assurances, if you will, of the hereafter. It's so…well, uninformed."

She began laughing, and not with him, for he was as stone faced as he had ever been. Her levity was not directed at what he had professed. No, she was clearly laughing at him. Clearing his throat, he continued.

"Well, just as some make stories of visiting loved ones to comfort themselves when fearful, others laugh and make light of the truth." He refused to sneak a glimpse of her face as he said this, although he wanted to look again at her lips. *I could kiss those all day and night.*

"Oh my, we have lost our humor." She stepped quickly ahead and turned to face him, causing him to stop short of bowling her over. "I don't get it. How come it's always the religious peddlers who don't believe in anything but what their religions teach?"

"And whatever does that mean?" He was really getting steamed but refused to let her know. He moved around her body block and continued on. Following, she continued.

"Look at what your faith teaches. Jesus died and rose from the dead. God, who happens to be invisible and all powerful, created the world, the universe, and all that we see. You teach that a Holy Ghost, hear that, ghost, lives in the hearts of believers. That those who die 'in Christ' go to heaven to live for eternity with God. Yet, someone sees a ghost and you take on the town with your haughty position that nothing like that could happen. Doesn't make sense." Her face was turned toward him but he could not look at her.

"I did not say that I believed or disbelieved the entire Christ myth or the more primitive understandings of the meaning of divinity. I simply maintain that these stories are not the historic presentation of reasonable, functional faith." He wondered if he was losing and had no idea how to regain his authority.

"Then I, as one who happens to believe in Jesus, would seem insufferably ignorant to the genius of you, my good Reverend. How enlightening." She was laughing at him again, and, for the first time in ages, he was amused by the exquisite trap she had set before him.

"What is your name?" he asked. "Your real name, now. I have a glimmer that it isn't Marilyn, nor Morgan, as you said before."

"Call me Mildred. No, call me Millicent. That will do." She was gazing at the sky as if listening to someone else. He followed her gaze and saw only blue dotted by a few distant birds.

"Mildred or Millicent. Sounds like a name that one might give to continue to hide a real name. And with the same first letter one could almost believe that you would mix the two names up, especially when it is supposed to be your own." He felt confident the scales were slowly balancing.

"My name is Mary Ann, and that's the truth." She was still gazing up.

"Do you live here? I've never seen you before, well, I guess the first time was about two weeks ago."

"I am staying with friends nearby - the Alles over on Circle drive. I used to live here but left suddenly…" The last sentence hung in the air as the gliding birds did so far above. A chill touched the back of Rev. Sinclair's neck. Something was strange here.

She thrust ahead, "Reverend, I find it hard to believe that you always understood your faith in these terms. You seem so involved with meaning and symbol and the human experience. Calling Jesus a myth is no accusation to easily overlook. To minimize a God that has been acknowledged for millennia is also quite significant. And to do this in the name of higher education is, well, arrogantly ludicrous. Yet, you've captured the minds of the entire community and the believers in ghosts are quiet. So much hard work to tear down what others believe with little effort in providing something better. Were you always this way?"

He did not want to tell her that he had believed greatly all his life. His dear parents modeled the quintessential Christian family for his siblings and himself. They loved him, nurtured him, and provided for him sacrificially. He and the other Sinclair children never knew they were a struggling family as his parents filled the material vacuums with adventures, faith, and their ever present support in all they did. Nor did he want her to know that in college he received his "call" into Christian ministry through the work of a small community social service center. He so related to the independent Baptist pastor who often volunteered at the center. The man's faith was as clear and honest as spring water, his intentions were simple as well - he lived to help others live a bit better.

In the midst of a nation's struggle for purpose and meaning during the Viet Nam war, he had found his direction in the call that God placed on his heart. With great pride, his entire family, and his old church back home, made sure that his call became a commission of faith. It was the intermediary step that caused him his significant theological shift from belief to a sort of spiritual rationalism. Seminary, the boasted fount of faithful learning was, in truth, a challenge to all he held dear. He entered a man filled with hope for a better tomorrow with God's help. He left a suspicious cynic convinced that all humanity was being afflicted by the unrealistic claims of a faith journey not accurately understood. Point being - it really did not matter if God existed or not. The true value of God was in how our behavior was enhanced by finding some abstract understanding of he/she/it. This "personal God" motif, he felt, was nothing more than a thinly wrapped adornment on the true God/gods explanation of life. Meaning, who the blazes knows and even cares.

No, he certainly did not want her to hear of his faith found, revised, sifted, and lost for the psycho/social gospel he now preached. But he told her. Every bit of it.

After his catharsis was completed, she walked with him for a long time in silence. Finally, before cutting again through the woods, she whispered, "It must be very dark for you in the night when you are alone in your bed with nothing but your blankets and your dogma."

He watched her disappear a little too quickly as she made an abrupt exit down a wooded trail. He found himself wanting to follow her but powerless to pursue. He felt empty and decided he needed to eat.

That night he found no sleep.

It took only a month for the fervor to still and the talk of ghosts in the lake communities to wane. Perhaps a few unreachable stragglers were still indulging themselves with these fantasies, but no longer was it the news in the aisles and parking lots of the church. Rev. Sinclair accepted the accolades of his colleagues, as well as other community leaders, in his single-handed campaign to bring reality back into the valley. Sadly, however, church attendance was down considerably and his acquaintances from church invited him to fewer social functions than he normally enjoyed. But he knew folks were busy, as was he.

His greatest disappointment was that Mary Ann did not come around. Glimpses were caught of her meandering through wood and yard, down one road or across the lake. But never close enough to visit with her. He did want to tie up some of the loose ends of their visit, but the opportunity was not presenting itself.

Cleveland TV learned of him, as did the local radio shows. Soon, his local celebrity was shared with northern Ohio viewers and listeners. A major Ohio magazine picked up the story which then led to a brief mention in Time. Newsweek clamored for the follow up, listing him as one of a number of national pastors dedicated to the reform of faith in the new century. A major publishing company sent him a proposal for a book on "The New Faith," as they called it. He was floating on the opportunities, as well as the notoriety.

As summer ended and fall beckoned with continued warm nights but changes in the light of late afternoon, Rev Sinclair began noticing a slight reddening of the maples and a browning of the oaks. He noticed he was often alone. Rev. Sinclair, man of faith for the new age, was not feeling very prophetic or apostolic. Actually, he felt empty. In his emptiness, blue gingham seemed linger in the shadows.

He came upon Mary Ann again during a walk on those rare days in late October in Ohio when all is baking hot and breezy but the colors are exploding from the surface of each leaf and meadow grass. His walk seemed illuminated by the dying cries of beauty the summer's foliage offered him. Suddenly, she was there at his side, the same blue gingham dress on her still youthful looking body. She, too, was radiant.

"Seen God lately?" she began. "I hear he was seen in the face of a newborn. Thought you would want to know."

He wondered what that was supposed to mean. It was good to be walking with her again.

"I see God in everything," he pontificated, "and in everything there is God, for we create God in our appreciation of the random-ness of nature." She started to rebut but he placed his hand on her arm and smiled as he said, "I was just kidding. Thought you might like a bit of seminary with your cynicism." They laughed together comfortably as old friends looking through pictures of a vacation shared many years ago.

"I think that perhaps I may be finding God again." He quietly ad-mitted. "I ran into a former parishioner at the Dink's Colonial Diner and he he was telling me how sad he was to graduate college and move home, leaving behind the exciting church he attended on campus. He was not pushy, just filled with some light I have not seen in a long, long time. I realized that I remembered how being in that 'light' felt.

"I also found that there are no Alles on Circle Drive. No living ones, at least. In fact, it has been years since the Alles family inhabited the Paw Paw valley."

"I know." She responded with confidence, offering nothing more. The Reverend resisted the itch to press her for more.

"It feels good to believe, again. I had wandered far without even knowing it. I really appreciate that you came." She said nothing, but walked slightly closer to him.

"Will you be leaving soon?" he asked with sadness in his voice.

"Yes and no." She already looked less substantial. "I will always walk these lakes, but you won't see me. I don't think I'll be able to see you either. But I am part of this." And she swept her hand over the meadow and lake. "There was concern about you and I guess I was called up to help out — me already being here and all."

"I understand and I so cherish our visits. I'm already starting to change in small ways. It would do no good to flatly and immediately convert. I fear it might confuse the congregation that "I once was lost but now I am found" as the old hymn says."

"Ya know Al," she said. "That sounds like a good plan."

Bemused, he gave her a glance just knowing that she knew he had never gone by Al in his life.

"Thank you." He wiped a small tear from his eye and looked into the heavens. It was so bright and clear. He imagined he could see all the way to heaven and beyond, and, in a small way, he could.

She seemed to fade somehow as they continued on. As she turned to a path in the forest, she reached over and touched his arm, penetrating his flesh with her caress of spirit. His breath skipped in a staccato jump of joy and wonder. Then she was gone, once again moving out of sight into her private shadows.

That night, as he said his prayers for the first time in ages, he found a new comfort quite unexplainably close. Turning to his stomach and reaching his arms under his pillow his fingers came upon a corner of his top sheet that, in his mind's eye, felt amazingly like he imagined blue gingham might feel. And he slept.

Agnes' View of the World

Life had been less than regular for Agnes Eisenberg. The only thing it had truly given her was prolonged years of dissatisfaction and pain. Beginning with a childhood of grief and agony and continuing with a marriage to a man who was ambivalent, at best, for the years of her marital incarceration. They spawned children who grew up and left her, visiting rarely and always briefly. Even her faith, as the daughter of a cantor, was as old and brittle as her dry, colorless hair. Nothing in this life gave her any desire to discover whatever any afterlife might hold.

It was the regular life of one whose life was just gray.

She had learned to avoid joy, for in her younger years it tried to change what she knew about life. Joy was a devious servant of cosmic forces which tried to make one forget or ignore the realities of despair. She was not going to be fooled by the smile of grandchildren or the call of an acquaintance for tea. No sir. She was a devoted attendant to the truth that life held little. Especially for her.

The persistent maintenance of her insipid lifestyle had, unfortunately, jettisoned almost everybody who might have attended to her. Agnes saw herself as a responsible human who had the duty to illuminate others about this wretched human life we all share. However, the others who drifted into and out of her life all seemed unappreciative and resentful toward her for bestowing of the Real Picture, as she referred to her despicable life, to all she knew. Obligation rested heavy upon her to disseminate the seeds of life's hazards to everyone she encountered. As a result, she had been left very alone in life, even when married.

Ritualistically, Agnes sat in front of the picture window of her small home on Paw Paw Lake. Her home overlooked the lake proper and at one time commanded a coveted view of the water. Of course, a house had been built directly across from her home, largely blocking her view, but that was an expected matter of policy in the preamble of how life really was. Why would a house not be erected in the center of two thirds of her panoramic vista? In actuality, she had always been surprised that a house had not been put up to block her view years earlier. Even in this, she saw just another misleading joke that was a parable of life in the Real Picture.

On both sides of the obstructing house, she could see the lake and the trees and bushes which surrounded the waters like a scarf around ones neck on a chilly morning. Geese, with their vile and unending black marble-like droppings, and smaller animals occasionally came into view. She'd watched many seasons pass from that window and had observed the numerous states of the lake from her perch. Not much to see, really. Just woods and water. But it did help time pass. And what else was there to do? Watch TV? Read? Pah- such occupations were for those who could not face their lives, desiring to fill it with diversion in the name of entertainment. But not Agnes. She was determined to face each day of her life has she had each previous day.

Mostly, Agnes just sat and thought. And bitter thoughts they were. She turned thoughts of her childhood, with its school and forced play with others, with its study and learning, over and over again as one would flip hash brown potatoes. Thoughts of her family - those with whom she was forced to live, with their holidays and Temple and pets and traditions. Being forced to go on trips and visit aunts she detested and eat picnics which always seemed to lodge in her windpipe, choking her with sentimentalism and cloying kind words or good intentions. Thoughts of her marriage to Ruben, the dolt she finally took as a mate to get her family to leave her alone. Ruben was a "blessing," as if she believed in such nonsense, because the family didn't approve of him. They were Orthodox and he was Reformed. She showed them all.

Then kids came. Five kids to watch and feed and truck after - with their demands and longings and troubles. She had a baby almost every time she had sex. Life was unfair and that was certainly life. No masking the obvious for her.

If you didn't know her, you might have thought she was acrid or harsh from birth. Almost as if she had a dour perspective of life from the womb. But you would be wrong, for Agnes began life as a deeply loved child to attentive parents who cared deeply for her. It was around age three when her mother introduced an interloper in the form of a cherubic infant brother that she learned that big people will talk about sour milk more passionately than fresh milk. Reality became severe when parents betray, and few were as brave as she to defy it without distraction.

Now, she just went on, day after day, in search of her end.

She inherited this house from Ruben, along with his money and pension. Plenty to live on for all she cared. She rarely went out and simply paid Geauga County Senior Services for most of her needs. Necessities were brought in by bleeding heart groups like Mobile Meals and the county Services for the Elderly. The attendants always tried to cheer her up, as if cheer was anything within the sphere of what she might want. She gave them "her look" and sent them packing. No need to be so indulgent with fools. She was paying them wasn't she?

Sometimes one of her kids would call to "check in." She knew they were waiting for her money. They'd be surprise when they tried to get it. Her will was well thought out and specific. She's left everything to the county waste treatment plant. Now wouldn't the papers like that!

Agnes was very old; ironically ancient as a matter of fact. She knew death couldn't be too far away. But she felt no concern. When it's done, it's done. She kept her mind from wondering and she built great walls which towered far above any regrets that might try to come through. This is what one did in a regular life.

In her last months, however, some things changed which deeply bothered her. In truth, she was slightly moved by these events, almost wishing she could allow herself to consider their meaning. She knew she wasn't mad or senile, or even slipping due to bad health. Like Moses, she knew she'd be healthy when death came, requiring that she give up her life herself, as the Torah said that Moses did.

Lately, it bothered her that she had started seeing ghosts.

Regularly.

It started with a spectral procession from the lake, through her neighbor's yard and right through her property. They came in silence as white-blue apparitions, walking painfully and slowly. These spirits would disappear as they came in contact with her house, leaving her a good view of the next in line.

Now, make no mistake here. She was scared and terrified and quite troubled by it all. They came alone but in long rows. Some were people she knew and others she had never seen before. Some were in faded costume and muted color and others were goofy looking like that cartoon, "friendly ghost," being spectral. It seemed the procession never tired, day in and day out. And it all bothered her greatly.

Agnes was paralyzed by indecision about what to do. She had no friends, and who could be trusted with such stories of ghosts? She wasn't going to start praying this late in life. What had God ever done for her? Call her kids? And they would run to the judge to have her put away so they could settle her estate into their savings accounts. She was on her own with this one just as she had been alone in about every other thing in her life.

She could not remember how long they processed, or how many came to her. None acknowledged her, not even with a glance. They just moved on toward her, disappearing at the last, like some strange and unholy train.

The fools driving along or out walking dogs and the like didn't see the caravan of the dead as they walked across the road. The cars would just run through them and go on as you please. She noticed once that when that annoying neighborhood jogger, Rick Something-or-other from some Eastern European country now taking American dollars by teaching at the University, passed through one of the ghosts, he seemed to falter a bit and pulled in the hood strings of his sweatshirt as if he'd suddenly gotten a chill. Agnes bet he did at that.

Her thoughts swarmed around something in her mental bee hive that questioned how could such a thing be? Especially for her? She could care less if there were real ghosts or not. Wasn't too overly concerned if there was a God or a Cosmic Toaster in the heavens, so why waste cerebral energy with the mysteries of the spiritual realm. Blast it all, this was intolerable. But she was too afraid to jump from her seat and give the ghosts her say so.

So she sat there. And she endured.

At times, as they marched toward her hour upon hour, day after day, they would all suddenly disappear. The whole string, extending down to the lake, from which they seemed to be birthed, would blink out of sight and she would be alone again. When her heart eventually slowed down to a normal pace, she often cried in silence and would go to bed.

Once she saw a ghost as it sat at her breakfast table and studying her dilapidated barn through her rear window with great interest. She dropped her tea cup upon seeing him there, but he didn't turn or note her presence. She took detailed note of him though.

He (or was it an "it" – do ghosts retain their gender?) was in uniform although no weapon could be seen. He had long, gray gloves, which extended to his forearms, and knee boots. His clothes looked old and the pants had no pockets. An emblem of two hand swords, crossing each other, was stitched onto the arm of his upper sleeve.

He had a bushy beard; his hair was wavy and disheveled. His gaze drifted back and forth along the barn, as if expecting someone to come out from behind from either side. Occasionally, he would move, shifting his seat on the chair or leaning an elbow on the window sill, all seemingly natural and not movements of a specter.

Agnes could almost see through him, but he was not quite transparent. For a few moments, the sun came through the mid-morning cloud cover that so often dominated the northeastern Ohio skies, and illuminated her checkered red and white table cloth, passing through him. He somehow made himself more solid, blocking the light by solidifying. Yet, in his greatest efforts he still waned from time to time, not able to remain ghostly, let along substantive.

Then he was gone.

The night ghosts were the worst, all glowing and clearly able to be seen in spite of the darkness of the night. They would trouble her the most, probably because she was tired. They might sit in her chair or on her dresser. They might float at her side or above her. Sometimes she heard their breathing but mostly they were just there. The night ghosts always seemed to be watching her. That made it hard to sleep.

Her days were only broken by getting mail from the rusted, beaten box at the corner of her driveway. She would watch to see if she had received any mail but most always it would be a bill or flyer for carpet cleaning. If the white Postal Service pill box truck stopped at her mailbox, she'd get a cane and amble out. The most terrifying ghost had been the one inside and staring at her when she opened the mailbox door. It was just a head, glaring at her from on top of her electric bill. Before disappearing, it mouthed her name, just once. Then it was gone.

A less honest woman would have died of heart failure with these ghosts about. But even in her moments of terror, Agnes scoffed at them and continued on. A less forceful woman would have moved or called someone for help. Not this woman. She was not going to be undone by something that didn't exist. Life was regular, and so was she. She endured as she always had.

Agnes was found dead in her home. The postman had noted her

mail was not being retrieved and the pile was becoming quite large. He knew that the woman was very old and probably fragile. He called the South Russell police to report the pile of mail and requested that she be checked on.

The responding officer, Andrew Ramsey, knocked at the door, waiting for an answer. Following procedure, he knocked a second, and a third time. Returning to his car, he radioed the dispatcher that he was going to visually inspect the house through the windows. Shading his face, he looked in through the windows of the downstairs bedroom and kitchen. He could see nothing unusual, except a broken tea cup on the linoleum in front of the stove. He saw nothing unusual in the second bedroom. The small window, presumably the bathroom, had the white cotton curtains drawn.

As he rounded on the front picture window, he muttered a curse. The ornamental bushes in the planting strip had prickers on them. Carefully he made his way through and faced the window. As he covered his eyes with his hands to reduce the reflective glare of light on the windows, he became conscious that his view was blocked. His eyes took a moment to focus and he realized he was looking directly into the decomposed eye sockets of a shriveled and decaying human face. With a scream of shock, he pushed away and landed, in full force, within the bushes, piercing his body on the spines of the thorns. As he rolled, seeking to get further away from the ghastly remains, he glanced again at the horrible sight. The old woman's mouth was open in an eternal scream, her false teeth heaved forward just beyond her withered lips. Pulling aside his gaze, he crawled and hopped, finding it impossible to stand, to his cruiser to report the discovery.

The coroner determined the body had been dead for weeks, maybe more. Forensics found no evidence of foul play. It was ruled a death by natural causes. The body was removed and interred as stipulated by the will, which noted the appropriate provisions of her wishes.

Her family did not contest the will, strange and unfeeling as it was. The waste disposal plant manager decided to replace the feces aerator in the treatment plant with the windfall money, which was not an insignificant sum. The courts, however, did allow the family to remove the personal effects of the deceased for distribution among family members.

Agnes' few furnishings and valuables were taken, although few family members wanted mementos or reminders of the unhappy woman they hesitantly called mother. She was a cold, unaffectionate task mistress who had effectively trained her children from early on that any love would not find reciprocation.

As the house was being emptied, Lisa, the youngest, asked to be left alone for a few moments to walk the rooms in silence and contemplation. Before turning to leave, she caught a glance of a most curious phantom, strongly resembling her mother, sitting in the front room facing the picture window. The look on her face was one of fright and terror, as if she was seeing something horrible down at the lake. Then it was gone.

With a shiver, Lisa, too, departed.

Agnes watched them leave from her easy chair in front of the window of her little house. She had refused to answer the door and felt gratified to see them going. Nervy brats, coming unannounced in cars and trucks as if they were going to get something from her. No way was she going to acknowledge them. No sir.

She turned to face her obstructed view of the lake once again. It was starting again. Those souls were marching, ever so slowly, up from the lake and toward her house. Never acknowledging her, but ever advancing, they came, and came, and came…

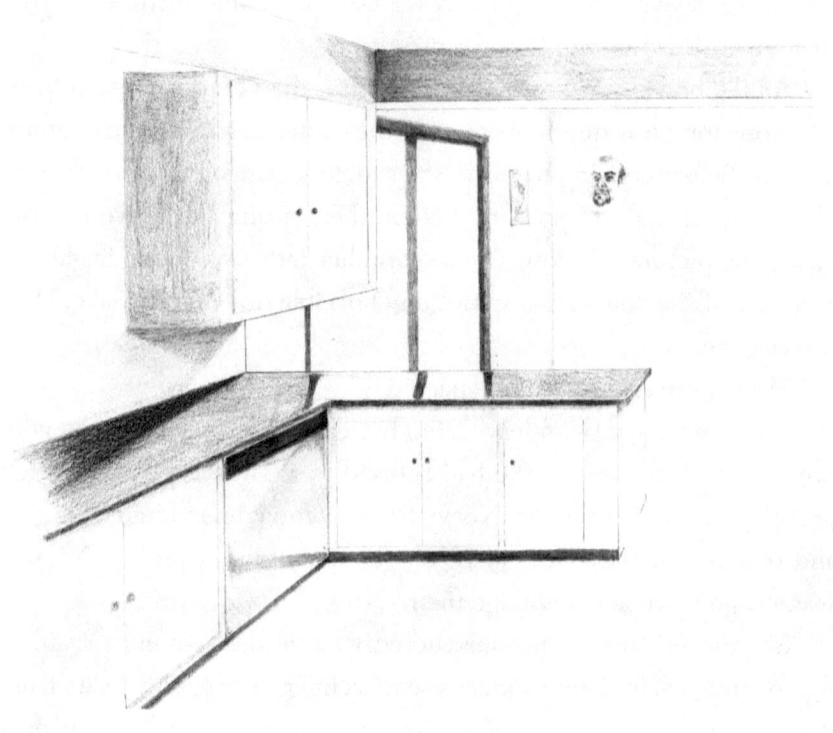

Evanescence

Sitting and watching TV in the darkness was becoming the new standard for romance for Janey Taylor and her beau, Stuart Kopechec. And that was OK because it somehow gathered together all of the favorite things they both miraculously shared - a mystical love of black and white, a passion for old fanciful love stories, cigarettes, and a lumpy couch that made you squirm and wiggle to smoosh down any of a dozen wads of misplaced cotton filler in the cushion beneath. The other benefit it offered was the excuse to get snuggly and closer.

Tonight Janey selected the movie, renting the Audrey Hepburn classic, *Roman Holiday.* Last weekend Stu brought a western that was actually a carefully disguised male bonding and relationship movie set in a genre of Yippee-Yi-Ki-Yo that guys could watch and not become embarrassed if they got all misty inside. As with every weekend, it was important together time for these two betrothed. A time to be quiet, bored and comfortable.

As the final credits rolled upward on the frozen, cloudy gray sky, they sat in silence. Janey hit the off button (on the front of the old remote-less set she had inherited from her grandpa) and they sat in darkness to conclude their two hours of mutual enjoyment by honoring the ritual of the fading of the single white dot in the middle of the screen as it drifted toward oblivion. The darkened screen crackled with static electricity. When all was black and silent, save the crickets still calling in the grasses outside the open windows, Stu cleared his throat; his signal that they had to talk.

Janey flashed back to her initial recognition of this "give away" sign that something important, as least of import to Stu, was now to be offered for discussion or debate. She recognized the sign from working with Stu for years in the InstantCare facility that offered quick fix health attention to the Valley residents. She loved it that they had known each other as friends before becoming lovers. Stu was head of Radiology overseeing a team of three. She was a nursing student paying for her education by working half-time as the insurance claims secretary, and then taking advantage of the innumerable insights she could gain by talking to the clinic nurses. They had known each other for quite some time and had been appropriately friendly in that inane, meaningless way that relative strangers are when a job forces them together, but not in any way that is beneficial to relationships.

During a bleak time of reorganization, with a looming buy-out becoming likely, the staff of all departments met constantly to discuss the rumors, the memos, and the suspicions in the lunchroom. Seating became assigned in the way that folks gravitate to the same seat each time they meet although it is unspecified. She and Stu had bought into that sociological concept and found themselves suddenly close in the meetings before and after work. She liked him well enough, and she became comfortable with his manner. Thus, she discovered his throat clearing prelude to conversation.

Stu began, "I have to leave earlier than usual tonight, Janey. Eric is going to give me a gratis exam in the morning before our Saturday regulars come in." Dr. Eric Hegedis was the weekend doctor on the team and the only doctor willing to barter for services. All the non-MD staff went to him for medical needs. She often wondered what he received in trade from his clinic staff clients.

"What are you giving him?" she asked as the thought traveled through her tired mind.

"Wha? Janey! That isn't the question one asks when one finds one's fiancée is having a checkup. One normally asks the reasons the other is feeling the need for an exam." Stu leaned over and kissed her nose. It was his "dear one" semi-patronizing gesture and she despised it although she would never let him know.

"Oops. I, the party of the first, solemnly beseech thee to forgive my blunder, oh party of the second, having only recently learned of these courting rituals." She rolled her head onto his chest and closed her eyes in a slight, but growing anxiety. "Why are you seeing him?"

"Just a checkup." He said.

"And..." she knew him better than that.

"And, to become more disciplined in my self-care. You know how we medical types can overlook our own medical needs."

"And..." she was slipping in for the kill. Men are so predictable.

A long and scary silence was broken by his trembling whisper. "And...I've had some blood in my stool." His chest shuddered involuntarily beneath her now completely awake head. *He thinks something is wrong* she thought.

They sat that way in the dark, totally silent, for a long time. Later, Stu went home. In her bed she turned her engagement ring around and around on her finger as she offered prayers for the morning's visit with Eric.

Stu called her at lunch, as he promised the night before, and told her that Eric thought he needed more fiber in his diet. Although his prostate gland seemed a bit large, he could find no cause for alarm. Both of them knew that hard stool can sometimes tear at the rectum and cause blood to be mixed on the outside of stool. For supper Janey promised him a plethora of nature's purest fruit in a collection of exotic and domestic treats. Stu made her promise to feed him grapes like in the gladiator movies. She asked him if he knew what "fat chance" meant, then she asked him if he knew any gladiator black and whites. It felt good to laugh.

Their wedding was a glamorous, albeit small, affair. She selected a traditional service of promise and piety in honor of her family's long heritage in the community of faith. He selected a wonderful variety of pre-service classical music featuring a string quartet, with *The Lord's Prayer* being sung by a soprano of unusual skill and depth. They wrote their own vows that were a beautiful pledge of all they felt and desired. The reception was held on the new deck they had built on her house that overlooked the forested side of Paw Paw. As a symbol of his confirmed good health, a secret only shared by the two of them and the best man, Dr. Eric, each table was laden with an imaginative variety of fruit. The party went long into the night and was the kind of gathering that makes other receptions somehow less due to the good company and celebration.

Early in the New Year, the blood returned to Stu's bowel movements and Janey sought counsel from a nutritionist to assure that their meals would assist his higher fiber needs. Eric gave Stu a stool softener help keep him comfortable.

One evening, in late March, Janey looked up from her nursing studies, rubbing her exhausted eyes to remoisten them. The self-massage felt so good that she enlarged the area, pinching the bridge of her nose and gently kneading her brows. She glanced at the clock and noted that Stu would be home in less than an hour. When he returned on his only late night, Thursdays in even months and Tuesdays in odd, he liked to have peppermint tea with her and to give her a foot rub. What a prince. She had never been able to turn him down, even though he was the more exhausted. Selfishness has its own rewards.

As she rose to put on the tea pot, she saw the ghost for the first time in the doorway of their small kitchen. It was a he, of that she was certain, but his image was too faint and undefined to reveal anything more.

She stood and stared, frozen but not consumed by terror as she would have believed, and watched the figure as it hovered before her. Her impression was that it was working hard at not completely fade out. It did after a few moments anyway. Releasing a breath she did not know she was holding, she returned to her seat and waited for Stu. Her eyes never leaving the door frame that had somehow sponsored her visitor.

Stu walked in the door, right on time, and called to her with promises of more than limiting his rubbing to just her two divine feet. He came to her through the same doorway through which she had seen their guest. Suppressing a chill, she told him of her encounter. He joined her at the table, at her side and together they watched the door. Stu felt unable to offer any proper response to such a claim as a ghost.

The next visit was about a month later, on a Tuesday night and under many of the same circumstances as the previous sighting. It was Stu's Tuesday month and she was, again, entering the kitchen to put on the tea when she walked right through the specter before seeing him. The moist chill and the immediate knowledge on some indescribable primitive level that it was again there caused her to drop the book that had engaged her attention and reel around to face what she knew would be there.

This time it was a bit more defined. Again, it was facing her with that strange sense of struggle and exertion.

She was calm, after settling down from the initial shock of his return, and tried to study it. It was the kind of ghost that we all seem to carry within; the shared ghost, in the classical, stereotypical, comic book, legendary style. Not quite Casper and far from Marley, but completely ghost and entirely real. There was no self-argument or denial. It was there and she was seeing it. Glancing at the microwave, she read the green numbers on its keypad clock and estimated that Stu was still a good 20 minutes in getting home. Perhaps if she communicated with it/him, it/he would stay until he arrived.

"Can you speak?" she hoarsely whispered.

He remained before her but offered no indication that he could hear or even see her.

Desperate to fill the air she began to tell him of her life with Stu and their dreams and hopes for the house and anything else that might pop into her overly stimulated mind in hopes of keeping him there. As she was running out of effective babbling, a realization struck her. It must be a ghost from a previous owner.

"Are you here because you died here?" she inquired. "Were you murdered here or did you build this house...Or maybe you died here and became a part of the place." She was struggling to remember her ghost lore. Having been a complete non-believer in "spooks," as she had called them, only a month ago, she found her knowledge of specters was bleakly deficient.

The ghost seemed to fade outward, its whitish essence spreading in a circling fashion, like a hula hoop in slow motion, and then it was gone. She slumped against a wall and rubbed her biceps as she crossed her arms under her breasts. On impulse, she genuflected and crossed herself. Leaving the kitchen, she waited for Stu.

Stu looked tired as he entered the house. She had again forgotten their tea which tipped him off that something was up. Practically falling into a chair, he studied her as she fell over herself in description and speculation of their ghost. He had never seen her frantically pace before, to and fro across the kitchen.

"I haven't seen it yet so maybe it's more accurate to call him your ghost."

"But I thought we promised to share everything." She objected, on the edge of stress-induced anger.

"Ghosts are a bit beyond my realm of my cosmology." He said.

Irritated she spouted loudly "Then get a new one. I need you to be part of this." And she went to put on the tea. Smiling into his hands as he rubbed his 10 PM shadow, he went to help.

Over the months that followed, the ghost returned to Janey many times. She never actually got used to it, but she did see a change in her receptivity and attitude toward him. She no longer stopped all to watch him. After three or so times he was less novel and more a project. She studied him in chunks as she could allow with her nursing studies. Additionally, she believed she noted a stabilizing in his shape and form, making him easier to see and less likely to misread.

But it troubled her than the ghost never showed himself when Stu was home. In spite of her promise, the ghost was something they could not share.

On their first anniversary, Stu took her to Toronto to see *Phantom* and to impregnate her with their first child. Being medical types it was a planned excursion with its numerous purposes, all of which played together to make a splendid trip. Stu continued to look tired, especially now that the clinic merger was to become reality after these many months, and she could not hurt and disappoint him by refusing to try to have a baby. Of course, Mr. Rational that he was, it was a great time. She would graduate in December with what would appear to be a basketball under her long graduation robe, have the baby in late winter, and be back on the job as soon as she felt ready and willing. Children were important to both of them and, although relatively newlyweds, they were not getting younger having met and married in their very late 20's. In Toronto, they enthusiastically insured a successful conception by practicing many times over.

True to their efforts, Janey did flunk/pass her "quiz" in the toilet bowl urine test. She saved the indicator tube to show Stu, assuming that the latent doctor in him would delight in the newly discolored positive strip embedded in white plastic, like an art print in a frame.

Holding the home pregnancy tester on her lap, she awaited Stu at the dining room table with a casual eye on the kitchen doorway just in case the ghost dropped in. She decided that if it/he appeared, she would not tell it/him first about the test and let Stu be the first to know.

Stu came in very quietly with none of his usual fanfare and flurry. She could hear him shuffling around in the mud room off of the garage, setting things down and removing his shoes and fall jacket. How strange. He never paused to enter on his late nights, always barging in to see her as immediately as possible. She shifted uneasily in her chair.

Moments later, when he did round the corner into the room, he only glanced at her with a tinge of apprehension blanching his face. Usually he seemed to fill up some deep and empty void within himself as he took her in. She covered the pregnancy test with her hand and moved it off to the side of her chair, tucking it between leg and chair cushion.

Standing in front of her he blurted out, "Eric found cancer" before falling in front of her and burying his sobbing face in her lap. Apprehensively, she put her hand on his head and let the shock of his revelation flood over her. As her own eyes welled up, she caught the white form of her ghost in its place in the doorway. It did not dawn on her that this was the first time it came to her when Stu was home.

In the months that followed all of the predictables occurred. Stuart Jonathan Taylor (her maiden name) Kopechec was born three months to the day following her graduation. She was promised a job as Eric's nurse at the now renamed QuickCare Clinic when she was ready. Stu's cancer was real and working hard to sink its teeth deeper into his system. It was a slow spreading variety, but, so far, he was having almost no success with treatments.

The ghost was still visiting her regularly, but never when she could show him to Stu. Since the night of Stu's confession, a confession of knowledge he had held from her for many weeks she had discovered, her ghost occasionally appeared when he was in the house or nearby, but not at times she would want to show him. In fact, the "Big C" news seemed to displace their ghost discussions with the more important issues of their lives.

Stu's health slowly withered in the time that followed. It became necessary for him to cut back on work. Almost before her eyes, Janey watched him drop pounds to the hunger of the cancer. Dark and growing circles of deep blue and smudgy black were evident under his eyes. He had a slight shake to his hands. His skin became waxy and unhealthy. His clothes fit poorly.

Work and little Stuart helped him to fight the advancement of the disease. Janey inspired him to seek higher thinking than the all too easy wallowing of "pity thinking" some sick people seemed to develop. It was not denial that kept them from discussing if it was terminal or how much time he might have. It was love. Medical people have lots of comprehension; some things don't need to be discussed.

Hope is a precious thing, so the little family attended prayer services when healing prayers were offered in the same chapel where they pronounced their vows of marriage. A gentle priest friend and patient of Stu's invited him to be anointed with oil for healing. Small communities such as the Chagrin Valley tend reach out and embrace their own when such tragedies arise. Their lake community was especially caring, doing innumerable things to show love and grace.

Janey's ghost was becoming more defined and she sometimes found herself alone and studying him for longer periods of time than she was aware. He would still not talk, but he showed her an attentive mindfulness that was not evident in the early visitations. It was some kind of nonverbal communication of ghost body language, or psychic connection, or some kind of spiritual understanding. It was both ancient and new age and, somehow, a familiar comfort to her.

She accepted that Stu was going to die before another year. She would have young Stuart, and that was some part of him, but her anguish was immense and her heart was often heavy with fright. She let Eric know that she would not be taking that job soon. Stu's disability insurance policy allowed them some freedom to be together all the time now that he had to quit his job at the Clinic. She cared for him most of the time and accepted the Home Health Agency nurse who now came three times a week to help. She could have offered medical care as well as the nurse, but she found it more important to be wife as least at long as the disease was going to let her.

The ghost came almost daily now. He communed with her in silence, always encased within the liminal space of the doorway. Never entering kitchen or dining room, it appeared facing whichever room she was in. She knew him so well now.

Stu died one night in bed next to her. He left her peacefully. She held him and cried and cried. Little Stuart did not wake up at the sound of her tears. She grieved without distraction, kissing him a million times and telling him that black and white movies would never be the same. As the first pale light of the morning crept into her room, she remembered how they would watch the TV dot disappear in the middle of the screen those many nights they spent on that lumpy couch. The dot would slowly fade into the blackness of the screen ever so slowly.

In the pale dawn, she gently laid his head on his pillow and slipped out of bed as though not to awaken him. She still cried freely as she looked in on little Stuart in his crib. He had a thumb thrust into his mouth and his little butt was sticking in the air, his knees drawn to his chest beneath his body. He had abandoned his covers, kicking them to the bottom of his bed.

She went to the kitchen and called Eric to tell him of Stu's mild and peaceful passing into eternity. Over the phone, she heard him begin to cry as he promised to come over after making the necessary calls. Slipping the phone into its cradle, she turned to watch the kitchen to dining room doorway. She lowered herself to the floor to wait.

In the pale light of early morning, he came to her as she knew he would. He had tried to come so often but without success. It could be only a partial coming as he was still not yet completely there. But now, on this first day of eternity, he was there in his new fullness. He was now whole and undivided between the two realms.

He looked at his hands of mist and leaned over to examine his body of fog. His eyes were full of wonder and awe as he looked with fresh perspective at his world. With a shifting, inner-glimmer, he pulled himself to full height and stepped, for the first time since his original appearance to Janey those many months ago, from the doorway into the kitchen and began to slowly cross the distance between infinite time and his lovely, dear wife. And as he faded, she understood the meaning of the word evanescence as Stu fleetingly dissipated into vapor.

In Remembrance of Me

Alexandra Haverstock mourned the death of her mother deeply. It was a loss that would truly diminish her as a woman. She would no longer be as substantial as she had been. The depth of her deprivation was immeasurable.

She felt great comfort in the eternal condition of her mother. She had observed her departure into the light and believed in her mother's claim in the Great Hope and Matchless Reward. In truth, her mother was zipped into God's very bosom, snug and secure in her Maker's spirit grasp.

Another one gone, Alexandra thought in frightened quietness. *How much more alone can I become?* She puzzled. *And how many more remain?* These were the haunting questions of a troubled heart.

Watching her mother's death, Alexandra's mind drifted to the good priest who offered Last Rites to her mother along with Communion just this morning. His voice was strong yet gentle as he admonished her mother to think of Christ in this holy meal. Alexandra could still remember from her own Sunday school years learning that Jesus asked us to remember him in the Last Supper. To reflect, as we ate and drank, of what he did for us. Alexandra knew and remembered, just as she was certain her mother did. Even as her last breaths were being counted down, she knew that each one held devotion to Christ.

Too bad she was so sick. This priest did not know her. He did not know that her mother was not Catholic. Lindsay Ann Haverstock was something like tenth generation Congregationalist. She had been head deaconess and, upon the occasions when the pastor was absent from the church on Communion Sunday, she had offered the bread and cup to the gathered Followers of Christ.

It was all right that the priest did not know her mother was Protestant. He held love in his eyes for this dear one about to pass on. His gestures were kind in their intention and gentle. He even paused in his service to wipe her eyes which were brimming in tears of uncertainty that the dying so often have. They were believers - not Catholic or Protestant or of any sect. They were only His Children.

Later that night, her mama died, slipping into the next life as quietly as an autumn leaf caught on the lightest of breezes descends toward ground.

And a bit of Alexandra died with her.

Alexandra looked closely at her own hands and arms and feet. Her skin had always been the type that seemed to be transparent. She could see the blue veins and imagined that the muscles which lie beneath that rice paper covering were observable. She let her hands drop to her side as she left the hospital into the deepening night. She walked aimlessly as one without destination.

In time, she arrived back to her house on the lake. She watched the moon's dull reflection upon the still, serene surface of water. The night was still. The surface barely moved within the confines of the shore. It was a ghostly sight. Too quiet. Quiet as the broken hole in the soil which received her mother. She felt tears, but none were released.

At the funeral, she knew what the minister would say before he said it. It was always the same. The prayers. The Scriptures. The hymns of indeterminate hope. A eulogy. Perhaps a treatment of the journey we all take as we leave this world. There was comfort in those rituals. They held meaning for millions over the centuries, and would help those in the future. It was well and good - except for the cursed words of finality. The veiled challenge. The feigned encouragement which was literally a pronouncement of doom on those who passed into death.

She imagined young Father Daiv in his black robe and long face as he exemplified the proper mixture of sadness, loss, and reflection so well rehearsed. He would pause as his remarks came to an end, look longingly among the gathered mourners, and quietly, with practiced emphasis and moving diction say, "And is it not true that as long as we remember Alex, as long as we hold the memory of her goodness and service in our minds, she will never truly die? So keep her alive, dear friends, in your thoughts. For in doing so, she will never truly be dead."

Of course, in Seminary they never teach you that the absence of those memories spelled the final death. They teach life eternal and unending. This thought that we are never truly dead if we remember. This was more than simply the good pastor's poetic device.

Who will remember me, wondered Alexandra, *now that mother is dead?* She again looked at her nearly transparent hand. *There are so few left who knew me.*

Alexandra walked on into the night. She crossed highways. She passed through homes of those eating, listening to music, making love, cleaning out the cat box. She drifted above the roof lines of the grain mill on the Chagrin River as it cuts under Main Street, and the noble Chagrin Hardware. She perched atop a bank and beheld the world of her capture; the place between where her mother had passed and the world of material and substance.

Once again she wondered who was left who remembered her. And, she wondered again, as she did so often now that nearly everyone she knew when she was alive was finally gone, what would happen when that last one who remembered her ultimately passed on to their own death. What became of those souls, such as she, who are not accepted into the light? Do they simply cease? Or are they accepted at the last? She did not know.

But she knew this utmost of discoveries could not be far from her in material and substance. For now, however, it was apparent that there was at least one who remembered her. And for that, she felt glad.

Colonel Brewster's Lakes

Since his boyhood, Emerson Herbert Brewster had been hunting these dense woods around the lakes of Russell Township for the game they rendered and the sport they provided. Coming from a family of farmers turned soldiers, as the times might require, he imagined his soldiering as he stalked his prey across field and through the undergrowth of the enormous woods that surrounded the area. When his turn came to enter battle, in the Big War, he joined his Pappy and G-Pappy in the Brewster tradition of hunting the enemies of our country and making sure they were put down. The Brewster Family had many stories to tell of its men folk and the battles they fought, both here and in Europe, dating back to the American Revolution. They knew how to aim a rifle and, when needed, how to extinguish a life.

Now, still favoring his right leg with its generous supply of shrapnel compliments of those enemies from across the ocean, he continued his life of hunting as he preyed upon the game so abundant in these parts.

His family had farmed, beginning in Virginia, since the Revolutionary War, or at least some time close after. Farming and warring became the defining insignias on each male Brewster's heart. And as the family spread, these two identities prevailed.

No one really knows when the first Brewster entered the Chagrin River valley to settle and make a life, but it was close to the original time when these lands became available around 1830. Records didn't exactly post dates when Brewster men removed trees to build homes and start farm lands, but family tradition claims Ezekiel Brewster came to the Ohio Territory after the War of 1812. The Colonel told all who would listen that the family name had been here since 1820 and something, but that is likely a decade too early. For Emerson's part, the Brewsters had come here damned early on.

As a boy, he would roam east of Chagrin Falls, a small community established in 1833. It was a tiny town consisting mainly of essential supplies dealers, located 40 miles or so southeast of General Moses Cleaveland's settlement which had been established along the mouth of the Cuyahoga in 1796 by the good general. Into this uninhabited area just south of Russell Township the Brewsters began their history in the Chagrin Valley. Originally, few farms had yet settled into these heavily wooded lands. It was just too overridden with forest. Why, he remembered his G-Pappy telling him that when his Pa, Emerson's great grandfather, started toppling trees and digging out stumps, a squirrel could jump into a tree and climb straight through to the western or eastern border of the state without touching ground once.

Over time, much of the rest of the county developed sprawling farms. And good producing farms they were, with live stock and fields full of corn and hay and wheat. It was a fertile land and more and more valuable as the farmers looked for new lands to develop. And yet, the Brewsters had reserved a plot of their huge holdings creating a mile by mile plot which they allowed to continue as natural as Mother Nature had made it.

So young Emerson would roam these lands unchallenged, drifting from trickle to stream to lake, each one unspeakably beautiful. Hunting, trapping, or simply exploring, in his mind these lands began to call him. As often as he could Em Brewster would tromp through the woods in search of whatever they offered.

Emerson never expected to see others on these excursions. On occasion, he would bring a friend or one of his younger brothers, but mostly he just liked coming alone. Often he would camp a day or two, always on the move. He discovered a couple of natural caves in his ventures and knew every fruit tree and berry bush. This was his real home.

Emerson knew the stories of the First Americans that had once lived here. As G-Pappy told it, they just disappeared over time, leaving to some other place, as pagan savages would when faced with the challenges of civilization. No loss to the community to see them gone was how G-Pappy held it. Secretly however, Em thought seeing an Indian might be pretty great.

Even with all the Native Americans now gone, Emerson dreamed of what Indian life might be like. To live among these lakes, counting on them entirely for food and water. To be at the mercy of the weather in daily survival. To live in a lodge with the tribe, tanning hides for clothing and shelter and using the gifts of the forest for cooking and heat. He imagined the night fires and watching the moon take its course across the skies, night after night. It was all too glorious, but he learned early on in life to keep such thoughts to himself. Parents took no kindness to idle-thinking youth who hesitated in chores and coddled to legends of the "native pagans" who had once lived in this township. His parents had no imagination of a simple, natural life.

As a young boy, Em saw only the displays nature held for him in these woods and among these lakes. Other humans would have been strangely unnatural. Which is why when he actually did see an Indian trekking through these woods, in his teenage years, it was such a dramatic and unbelievable sight.

It was in mid-winter while checking his trap line along the small streams which linked the lakes together. He had just field dressed a rabbit when he heard the snap of branch under what he supposed was the foot of a deer. He pulled his gun to his shoulder, remaining close to the ground, and thumbed the safety in readiness. A flash of motion in his side vision beckoned him. As he turned, he thrust the stock of his rifle deeper into his shoulder, lifting it to claim the animal. From habit, he continued the movement of setting the gun for a shot in a fluid motion, making ready his entire being for the one shot he might get off. Everything had to line up perfectly as the trees were fairly thick along this part of the stream. He'd only have one chance at a shot.

Two or three brief glimpses confirmed the position of the deer.

More intent on the shot than the animal, he fired the second he saw it in a small clearing, jumping to his feet when he saw it fall among the undergrowth. He slid the bolt of the Remington smoothly to insert a new cartridge into the chamber. Often the first shot only downed a deer for a moment requiring a second shot for the kill. Running toward the spot of his last glimpse, he confirmed his rifle ready.

Approaching the down site, he confirmed he had made a hit. The snow was splashed with blood and an imprint of a body was evident. A drag trail went deeper into the thick, brush-covered woods as the beast attempted its escape. Emerson slowed, rechecked his gun, and followed.

The path went along a narrow break in the heavy undergrowth, the apparent bed of an old stream or a run off for spring rains. No trees grew there, so tracking was easy. It twisted quite a bit so he could not see too far ahead. Blood droplets colored the white snow dramatically, leaving a radiant trail.

Speeding to a trot, he rounded a turn in the path and came to a halt as he saw his prey clearly for the first time. His knees felt weak and insubstantial as horror gripped his heart. He had shot a man.

His glimpse was too brief to show him anything more than the fact that his victim was struggling ahead on two legs, not four. With dusk coming on, he became concerned about helping the man to the dirt road far to the north. Wiping his damp forehead, he pressed on to help the wounded man.

He quickened his step and closed the winding distance between the still unseen man and himself. The path of the stream bed twisted and turned through the woods and began to ascent up a rise. He saw the man again as he limped over the top of the knoll. Unbelievably, the man was dressed as an Indian. At least as Emerson assumed an Indian might be dressed, entirely in tanned leather. Rational thinking fled the youthful Em completely. He could find no explanation as to why one would dress so strangely.

Over the small hill, Emerson saw the man as he rolled to a stop near the bottom. He had stumbled and, in his weakness, fallen with no hope of rising again. The crimson emblem on the furs of his over garment spoke of the severity of the wound. Slowing, Emerson approached the body.

The blood was so red, the snow so white, and the air so cold. Perhaps that was why his eyes erupted in uncontrollable tears. He felt a choking in his throat and fear as he had never experienced in his all too young life. The Indian, as he truly was, turned his head to face his killer.

No words were spoken. No help was asked or offered. As the light of the day drained, Emerson watched, transfixed by the pull of the other's eyes. He felt himself slipping into the intense, pain-filled stare of his unintended victim.

He knew he had killed, not a real person, but an intangible of some sort.

He also knew his fearing had just begun.

Snapping from his hypnotized pause, Emerson lifted the fur shirt and looked at the Indian's chest. The man offered no resistance. He was greeted by a confusion of mangled flesh and oozing blood. There was no help to offer. As the native pleaded with his eyes, Em worked to avoid his stare.

Into Emerson's mind would trickle thoughts of where this man came from or how it was that a First American would be here at all. His numb and tortured mind could not solve the strangeness of the scene. He could only absorb, in small doses, the reality that he had killed a man; a man of some other, much earlier century who was going to die before his eyes.

With a hand made bloody by trying to hold in his own blood, the stranger suddenly gripped Em's arm with a strength that belied the wound centering in his torso. In his language, he softly cursed Alex as an intruder who would find no peace in this world until the stations of life were changed. At least, that's how the words felt as Em heard them. As the Indian died, he faded from sight as the ghost that he surely and certainly was.

Emerson collapsed to the blood stained ground in a faint; lying unprotected upon the snow in the woods just above the lake.

Later, after it was fully dark, Em awoke in a panic, immediately remembering all that had happened. He lunged back from the place where he had last seen the strange Indian moving crablike through the heavy drifts, although it was too dark to see anything. It was as if, climbing from his swooning sleep, he still saw the Native American. His vision finally caught up with reality. No one was there. Gathering his rifle and closing his coat more tightly to the intruding cold, he returned to his camp, abandoning his traps, pelts and carcasses in the midnight of the woods.

As the night passed, Emerson, sitting by his fire, wondered if what he had witnessed had actually happened. His mind was tortured by the loathing that he had actually shot another human. He remembered the words he perceived as a curse and questioned how it was that he had understood the spirit of the garbled words. After a time he convinced himself that it was all a hallucination, likely sparked from too much time in the cold. However, it was tough to explain the bloody hand print on the sleeve of his coat.

Early the next day Em gathered his things and returned to his home, never speaking of his experience and the curse he felt had been placed upon him.

Over time, he thought less and less of the encounter. Life passed for him as it does for all young men starting out. He worked, met new people, spent some time in school, fell in love, had a first kiss, and more. In the early years of this century forces gathered in war in Europe and Emerson, like his ancestors, turned out to enter the battles that others had conceived. He fought for his country in countries that held strange customs, languages, and views of life. Often, in fox holes or in some base camp, he thought of his lakes back in Ohio. He wondered if families were beginning to buy up some of the farm land his Ma wrote was going up for sale by some of those unknown and absent owners. He dreamed of a nice, small house on the same lake at which he met and killed the Indian. That had a full circle notion from which he believed he could create some type of reconciliation.

Time passed, as time will do, and Emerson returned to his family homestead intending to get on with his life. Soon after, he met a lovely lady, Sophie, the daughter of prominent farmer and determined to establish his new family in their own home. While his father was not happy in Emerson's request, he was eventually persuaded to sell off the parcel of family owned land that was to be Em's portion of the farm. The proceeds of the sale were given to Emerson and allow him to buy a plot on one of "his" lakes. The owner was located and Emerson and Sophie became the first residents of Paw Paw Lake, in the new township of South Russell. The marriage began with promise but over time dissolved into the perfect warning of why people should avoid marriage.

Theirs was not a happy life of post-war adjusting and becoming established. Rather, it seemed that every day brought some tension, some suspicion, and some bitterness between the newlyweds. They focused on building their dream house, but seemingly always made decisions that were either unfortunate and uninformed, or just simply bad. Kids began to come, and they seemed to be mostly ill and not very close. Each family member had a veil of ambivalence for the other family members. Nothing was ever quite right.

Other residents began building houses along newly cut road that edged along Paw Paw Lake. Over the years Emerson and Sophie witnessed the birth of a lake community firmly incorporated within the natural foliage and forest of this beautiful lake. For Em, it was heaven – the only heaven he had ever known. But his heaven held a secret.

Emerson would hunt in the woods, just as when he was a more youthful man, and he took up fishing in the lake, a hobby which he had

had no time for while working back on his dad's farm. He would often look through the stalks of the forest in search of game or deer, or so he told himself. More than once, he wondered if the glimpse he caught of the Indian from his youth was real or imagined. Time so dulls the edges of even the most clearly traumatic memories.

He found work in the grain mill just north of the Chagrin River. It was a dirty job; his hair, clothes and lungs filled with the hull dust of his labors. He was promoted to manager over time, but that only brought him face to face with employee troubles. All in all, however, Alex thought that this was a pretty normal life and how life was for everyone. His life creed became *you get happiness or you get life — but you can never get both on the same day.*

Life became modern at a rapid pace after WWII and the whole face of the Chagrin Valley slowly began to change. Highways linked the outer communities to Cleveland and Akron. The company grew. Sophie began to drink maybe a bit too much. His kids talked him into getting a family pet for the house. A cat, of all things. Cats were for keeping the mice down in the barns, not sleeping on the sofa. Even the family pet represented irritation.

Emerson began what he called, in his mind, his slower years. In reality, he was mostly depressed. Graying at the temples, feeling the pull of gravity upon his limbs, he felt sluggish in his motions and manners. Yet, few days would go by without finding him trekking through the woods to the lakes he so loved.

Other communities went in around the sister lakes of Paw Paw. People moved in, putting houses up while trees and some of nature's finest fields went down. Alex took note but found that he wasn't as concerned as one might think. The fight had left the dog.

Other things occupied his thoughts. Other burdens and considerations. All the joyless days he had lived on this earth seemed to crystallize into one sighting. In one moment all of angry thoughts and numerous displeasures were met in the stare he remembered so well.

The stare of a dying man watching him.

It happened unexpectedly one fall evening when the colors proposed the undeniable coming of winter but the temperatures still said that summer was not going to retreat without a fight. Emerson was drifting through the woods behind his house, one of sixteen homes ringing the lake that was destined to hold just over forty in the future. When he emerged the thicket, he locked eyes with a man. Unknown to Em, this was the exact spot at which he stooped to field dress a deer so many years ago. There was the Indian, in the spot he had been that fateful day when Emerson noted his motion and made the shot.

Em looked at him and found himself paralyzed with fear and memory. How long they watched each other was lost on him. After a minute, or perhaps an hour, the Indian turned and traveled up the same dried stream bed that Emerson had trafficked that long ago evening. It was the same chase, hunter pursuing the wounded, as it had been before. The terror was not enough to detract him. Emerson knew he was destined to follow and find the Indian waiting for him in the spot of his ghostly second death.

The Indian waited and, when Em stood before him, he repeated the curse upon Em speaking directly into his mind and using his native language, still foreign to Emerson. The words of the curse reminded Em that the Indian had promised him no peace in this world until the positions were exchanged. In a flash, Em remembered all the bad years that followed the curse from the Indian.

For a second time in his life, the Indian disappeared. Emerson could not move.

That evening at home was marked by a sullen and distant Emerson. He wanted no meal from his wife and no distraction from his children. He simply brooded over the Indian's curse.

It was evident that the curse had been partially fulfilled in his life. While enjoying a murky success and finding life better than what he expected from death, he had not found the contentment that his various accomplishments might be expected to deliver. Peace had always evaded him after the killing of the apparent ghost.

Emerson had a sense of what might come next. He spent as much of his time in the woods as he could, always drifting to the place where he had seen the Indian before.

The years stacked up. More years than Em ever though he might live through. New changes forced their way toward a "modern" society. Young people became unpredictable, wearing colorful, patterned clothing that hurt his eyes and listening to music that was incomprehensible to his ears. Unrest became the motto of an entire generation. South of his area, in Kent, some students were killed on the campus in an anti-war demonstration. Gas became expensive, so did food. More lots were being sold around his lakes and houses were going up continually. The neighborhood kids were all grown and living all over the country. So were his kids. He had a couple of grandkids these days. Holidays came and went. So did quite a few decades. Gravity was pulling him; stooping his shoulders. He began looking forward to "his time" as most of his friends and acquaintances were finding theirs.

Yet death, just like peace, seemed to evade him.

Sophie died and was buried in what was left of the family farm up in Russell next to eight generations of Brewsters. Two of his children were buried by their mates in cities faraway. Em pushed on through life, never quite sure what awaited him.

The Indian returned to Emerson when he was quite ancient and close to crossing into a new century. He had few friends, little family, and no life other than his habitual shuffle through the woods near the killing spot of the ghost Indian. Questions of how such a creature could walk this earth and bleed when injured, or how it survived to haunt Em were never answered. He still caught occasional glimpses of his stalker through the trees, never aging, never allowing himself to be fully seen, and never speaking into his mind. *He's just passing a reminder,*

Em would sometimes mutter to himself.

It wasn't long before Emerson was found dead, lying in the snow along a small indentation in the ground left from some stream wash away near the undeveloped part of the lake. Quickly the crime scene officers determined it had to be murder. No clues, like shoe markings or finger prints, were found to aid the capture of the villain who murdered the gentle, quiet, and ancient man. In fact, if not for one curious bit of physical evidence, it might be ruled death by natural causes. His face sure looked peaceful, almost happy. Not the face of a man with an arrow of great age piercing his heart.

Birth of Decay

It's an awkward age, that space between "still young" and "getting old." And awkward is what Rand McGruder felt all too often these days.

He still ran as he had since high school. But his personal best 5:21 mile and 34:20 10k were considerably longer these days. He was still quite an attentive lover, but some days the "old soldier" just wouldn't salute. Same with yard work, backpacking and other pastimes requiring energy expenditures. He still could, but not as well.

47 was a stinker of an age.

Especially when it's the age of discovering that you have cancer.

Dr. Hegedis was more than the family physician. He was Rand's closest high school chum, college drinking sidekick, running buddy, and godfather to Hanna, Rand's youngest. He was also Rand's closest friend.

In fact, Rand's only kind of gay "almost" had been with Eric on a fishing trip when, after both had had way too much to drink, they got caught in a cloud burst during a hike in the hills near their campsite. Soaked to the skin, freezing from the cold rain they had stripped off their wet clothes, throwing them in the mud and crawled, entirely naked, into the tent. What alcohol compromised in their inhibitions, their "gay-dar" instincts had prevented. They just weren't gay but they truly loved each other. Laughing aloud they fell asleep, nothing happening. They remained comfortable, intimate friends, able to humorously "revisit" their near brush with contact. Now, eyes filling with tears, the doctor told the car dealership emperor the "what was what" about pancreatic cancer.

Rand felt as if he was standing apart from himself as he and Eric embraced and cried. He was there, crying and in Eric's arms of consolation. But he was also apart from the whole scene, totally un-attached from himself somehow. There was nothing latent about this clasping of two hurting men. This was the desperate clinging of two dear and devoted friends.

Leaving the office, Rand struggled with the questions of how he could reasonably process the new revelations which Eric had shared with him. What do you do with a death warrant bearing your name? How does one live with the slow intrusion of death? How do you eat breakfast with your kids and hamburgers with your employees? Or lead a sales meeting at his McGruder Motorcars? Or go to church? Read a novel? Pump gas? The details of life were suddenly and completely trivial and meaningless.

Rand drove slowly to Evergreen cemetery and sat on his parents' head stone, a combined job bearing both of their names and the dates of birth and death. The reddish granite, or marble or whatever rock they shaped and carved to make these memorials, was unforgivingly solid and lent a harshness to the visit.

Soaked to the bone, his clothes soiled from the wet ground of the grave, he lay, crying again, upon the snowy slush and leaf mixture of the early spring melt. Emotionally exhausted, he briefly slept above his parents as they rested in their own untroubled sleep.

Cold, wet, and dirty, with a streaky face and carrying the clinging organic debris of the cemetery, Rand rose and walked to his car. He spoke no words, thought or prayer to any parent, either earthly or heavenly, and drove home to Gwen.

Gwendolyn, his dear and loyal partner in matrimony, greeted him with their pet gesture somehow not seeing his demeanor. Tapping his forehead with her index finger she spoke their friendly, familiar salutation which they invented way back when Star Wars was still in the height of its rage.

"Heart of my heart, enter our domicile secure in my love."

Rand felt an overwhelming wave of love. Tears rose involuntarily as he completed his response, "I enter in devotion, Oh joy of my life." Sobbing he clutched Gwen, burying his face in her bosom. Comforting him she, too, cried and told him that a worried Eric had called to prepare her. Rand felt immense relief in not having to mouth the phrase, "I have cancer." Good ol' Eric.

Leading him to the couch, they wept together. In time, their two daughters, Jess and Hanna, joined the pain-filled huddle. Only Jakob, away in military service, was absent.

Days and weeks slowly passed. A final thaw removed the last snow in late April. Green shoots and buds adorned the yard and trees. Across the street and over the mild slope, Paw Paw Lake, the ageless and mysterious center of this community, shone in the sun, beginning to warm a bit each day; already inviting the children of the neighborhood to play near its edge.

Rand and Eric met often, both professionally and supportively. Reverend Horner, their priest at Grace Episcopal, had Rand and the family listed each week in the prayer bulletin. Mr. Kelley, the pharmacist, helped Rand to understand his medicines and carefully explained potential reactions. The McGruder family and their village friends established a new normal. A dying man walked among them. Was it impolite to stare?

Along the way of the budding spring, something in Rand's perceptions altered or adjusted. Or perhaps it simply fine tuned. What changed in him he never quite figured out? Nor could any explanation fully elucidate the events that accompanied his final months on earth. In short, somehow Rand developed some kind of other sight.

The first instance passed with Rand almost not seeing what he was seeing. While walking the lake path, which looped the lake through meadows and woods, Rand noticed three guys building a picnic table in the family play area up near the small cove which connected the lake to its stream source. Not wanting to be forced into a "friendly visit" with neighbors who wanted to say what Rand had come to call their "finals," he decided to slip by. He parceled these goodbye visits into tolerable and limited exchanges. This morning was not an "I'll accept visitors" morning.

Avoiding eye contact and keeping his gaze ahead and his pace strong, Rand quickly moved down the path. He secretly hoped to gain the curtain of the forest before anyone could beckon. In his peripheral vision, he could see the men swinging their hammers in the arching movements of confident builders.

A dozen steps beyond the tree concealment, he stopped in his tracks almost mid-stride. The staccato beating of hammer upon nail had been missing. Listening with rapt attention, Rand heard nothing save bird chirp and insect buzz. He reluctantly returned to where the table was being built. He saw no workers. The tables in the picnic area were not new after all. They were gray, weathered, and each of the three had a rotten, decaying top, badly needing replacement. In his overly challenged mind he was unable to absorb or understand what he was seeing now and what he had seen just moments before. He turned away, pushing the inconsistency out of his mind.

Three weeks later, he glanced through the window of the body shop area at his dealership as he passed on the way to his office. The guys were stooped over, working on the fender of the car brought in from a local accident earlier in the week. Moving past the small staff lunch room he briefly recounted that it had been totaled by the insurance company. Strange that Sammy, the body shop manager, would be spending any time on it. In his office he reflected at the amount of new business the body shop had added to the dealership since opening it a year ago June. Not only did the repairs bring in a good profit, but often when a car was totaled, the family needing a new car would give Rand a first chance at a replacement. Sammy paged Rand through Carol, his switchboard operator.

"Rand," began Sammy, "we can't tow this Lexus back after all. It has to be transported on a flat bed carrier. Both axles are so trashed that it will only drag if we yank it. Juan and I'll wait for City Towing, and then we're gonna catch lunch before we come back."

Confused, Rand asked, "Where are you calling from, Sammy?"

"We popped into Eddie's Bar out here at 306 and 422. The wreck is right out front. We ain't drinking Rand, if that's what you was thinking."

Sammy was a recovering alcoholic and was sensitive when anyone questioned his sobriety. However, that was not what was on Rand's mind.

"No, Sammy, I'm not worried about you being in Eddie's. I thought I just saw you in the bay, that's all." Rand thought that might settle Sammy.

"We're out on that Sheriff's Office call we got this morning. Mrs. Stallinger got nailed by a lumber truck what skidded through the intersection. She wanted us to get the car." Sammy paused. "Didn't Carol tell you we was going?" Now Sammy sounded mad. Mad was better than pouting.

"Umm. Hold on a minute Sammy." Rand said before placing the phone on his desk. He didn't bother with the hold button. He walked more slowly than might be expected back to the waiting room and gawked at the car that moments ago was being worked on by what he thought had been Sammy and Juan, his body shop crew. In the bay was a junker waiting its last haul to the scrap yard. Rand shuttered inside.

On July 4th Rand noticed during a morning walk that old man Toby Montgomery was finally replacing that rotted soffit and fascia that surrounded the roof line of his house. Rand had often wondered how the old fellow could live with the racket that the squirrels and birds must be making in those varmint infested overhangs. All that fluttering and prancing as they moved in and out of the gaps in those decrepit eaves had to be maddening. But good for Montgomery. He had two carpenters on it, replacing the rotted wood with new redwood. This little repair would improve the look of Montgomery's house and the entire street.

How did Monty find carpenters to work on a holiday? Rand wondered as he made his way home. *Must be a side job for some extra cash.*

That evening, as the community gathered down at the beach for fireworks, a party and cook out, Rand saw Montgomery and told him how great the repairs looked on his roof line. Montgomery gave Rand an obscene gesture and cursed him before heading back to his buddies in their lawn chairs on the end side of the beach. Throughout the evening, he and his buddies looked back at Rand often with scorn.

"I guess Old Monty didn't appreciate my compliment about his house repairs." Rand said to Gwen.

"Don't sweat it," Gwen encouraged. "Some people take nice comments and turn them into criticisms just to be ignorant." She turned back to her potato salad. Rand shrugged.

When the fireworks were over and the last beer can crushed underfoot for recycling, Rand, Gwen, and the two girls headed home the long way meandering through the neighborhood. Passing Montgomery's house, Rand was shocked to notice that the bare, rotted wood remained as it had for years. The house and yard lights illuminated the gaping holes and falling trim boards. Gwen followed his gaze as she asked haltingly, "I thought you said he repaired that mess?"

Still staring Rand muttered he must have been mistaking. The night took on a sudden chill for Rand as he and his family returned home.

In the months to come, Rand saw frequent and regular instances of these illusions. Sometimes he'd see two different occasions in a day. Other times it would be nearly a week and he would see no apparitions, which is what he finally admitted they must be.

In time, he put together a few apparent facts which seemed to be consistent with each visitation. First, they only occurred in the valley and within three or four miles of his home.

He never recognized the persons he saw in these visitations. They all looked like regular folks, but never anyone he actually knew.

If he looked away, even for a second, and then turned back, the vision, for that's what it must be, would be gone.

Finally, each sighting was of people in the process of building or making something; creating, so to speak.

He witnessed the building of the fireplace and chimney at Grover Farm, a farm that had been abandoned and was now in advanced decay. He watched as a crew of Amish men stained the exterior of the Stone Furniture warehouse out at the end of Gladys Street. Since the old barn was way off the beaten path, the Stone brothers hadn't bothered with repainting it for years.

Sometimes the "seeing" would involve structures which had been removed, like the train bridge down by the roller skating rink. The unused trellis had been torn down a few years ago amid public outcry insisting that it was an historic and beautiful structure. The railroad felt it was dangerous and an eyesore, and pushed the safety aspect to prevail. The old bridge was entirely disassembled and carted away in one day by cranes and more than a dozen workers.

When Rand saw it, a different dozen men were connecting huge "I" beams to the hangers on the concrete pillars which supported the bridge. He knew that when he passed, they would all disappear.

After the confusion surrounding old man Montgomery's over-hangs, Gwen noted Rand's occasional, prolonged gazing at similarly dilapidated edifices. She remained silent, but she wondered what his thoughts were. She determined that his own dying made him aware of other "deaths." She mourned in regret as she watched him scrutinize so solemnly.

Rand had already worked a deal to sell the dealership to a large automotive firm that specialized in "dealership collecting." Gwen was a lawyer, not a business woman; the kids had no interest in his offer to give it all to them as an inheritance. In mid-fall, Eric notified Rand that the cancer was progressing and told him he should "retire" as soon as possible. Rand inadvertently stung Eric with a "retire so I can expire" retort. Eric silently understood the crude deathbed humor.

Rand was bedridden for Christmas, the cancer now killing him at an alarmingly rapid pace. He accepted hospice care, hoping to die at home, and signed off his rights to heroic efforts, refusing everything but painkillers. On Christmas afternoon, Rev. Horner and his wife Cathy visited. As they prayed together, Rand knew he would not see the New Year.

That evening, after Gwen made him a wonderful fire and moved him to the living room sofa, Rand decided to tell her what he had been seeing since spring. Amid the colored lights of the tree, with Bing Crosby crooning Christmas songs softly in the background, he told his beloved of all of his visions. She listened, initially in concerned disbelief and then with a comforting understanding as he related the changes in his ability to actually "see." She remained silent until he was finished.

Intuitively she asked him what he thought of it all. Rand told her the similarities he had noticed; those combining factors which somehow unified each "seeing" with the others.

Gwen was silent for a long, long time, watching the fire and holding Rand's slightly chilled and clammy hands in her own. She prayed silently and then she spoke her observations.

"Hon," she began slowly, "it seems to me that you're witnessing the birth, in a sense, of things dead - or dying. You seem to be seeing the …ahh, original builders or manufacturers who made the things around us. And it's mostly stuff that we so easily take for granted, but that are also on their way out. Does that make any sense?"

Rand physically jolted with the realization of what she had said. It made total sense, somehow.

"So, I'm not seeing ghosts, per say." He offered. "I'm seeing the creations of the stuff."

Abruptly, he quit talking in awe of what he was thinking. Both remained in prolonged silence, mesmerized by the flames of the fire and the possibilities of the moment.

Gwen broke the silence. "No Rand, I sort of think you are seeing ghosts." She paused for some minutes before continuing, "No, no, not ghosts actually, but some kind image of the dead guys on these things they originally created. You remember that those picnic tables were all built by the three Stouffer guys - grandpa, who built the house near the turnaround at the end of the street, along with his son Earl and his grandson, Charlie Stouffer. They all died up in Canada on that fishing trip. Remember, they ate something bad and were poisoned. They died before they could get out and get help."

Thoughtfully, Rand remembered, "And Mr. Montgomery's house was built nearly 60 years ago. Maybe longer by now."

"The storage barn out on Gladys has got to be pushing a century."

"And that train trellis was put in by the WPA workers during the Great Depression," Rand said, "Remember the bronze plaque the village put up a few years back? All those guys must be dead. It's been too many years."

"And I'll put a million bucks on the bet that somehow the two guys you saw in the shop at work are also both dead."

Rand nodded absently. He was seeing the ghosts of those who made their places in the world at the time when their creations are heading for their own demise. Although puzzling and spooky, it somehow made sense. It was a cosmic impossibility that was his personal miraculous reality. But why?

That evening Rand remained on the couch. He was too weak to move upstairs. Before she went to bed, Gwen set up a baby monitor borrowed from a neighbor so that Rand could call her if needed. He asked her to stoke the fire before retiring and to throw on a few more logs. He felt quite awake and thought he'd watch the fire as he made some attempt to think of all they had discussed. Gwen left the Christmas tree on to cheer him. He was such a little boy around the lights and decorations.

As the house got quiet and settled, a final apparition appeared to him in the light of hearth and tree upon the Oriental rug which was before the fireplace. This time, one of the assumed rules of the specters seemed to be violated. Rand recognized the two naked lovers lying before him in an embrace of passion. With no embarrassment, he watched as his own dead parents made love. He could not look away.

As he fell asleep sometime later, he marveled at the miracle he had witnessed - for Rand McGruder had beheld something no human had ever seen before. He had watched with reverence as his own dear and loving parents shared their bodies and spirits in the ultimate expression of love. He had watched them as they created him. And in his last breath before his own decay, he understood.

Mrs. Randolph's Porch

The house is fairly nondescript and altogether unremarkable. It is a medium-sized family home on Main Street in a small New York community of passing affluence. The furniture industry came and went, leaving some demonstrative homes of astounding character. This is not one of those.

This house is well groomed and maintained. Fresh paint makes the occasional ginger bread adornments stand out. The lawn and grounds trimmed and weeded. It is a clean looking home of burnished yellow, almost ochre in color with white trim. Yet, were it not for the porch, which is extremely unusual, the house would be one of millions of other easily forgotten homes in America.

Any motorist headed for Randolph could not help but pass the house on Main Street. Although located at the beginning of Main, just off the highway which too often leads potential viewers speeding past the town, it is well out of the more residential areas. It stands among a few other homes in this outpost part of Randolph.

But to pass and not notice the porch of this Randolph home would be a sorry admission of either drunkenness or needing a visit to the optometrist. For the house of the woman we refer to after the town of her birth, Mrs. Randolph, is more a stage than a simple residence.

Mr. Randolph, who is said to own the local lumber yard, built the porch to his wife's specifications, with steps that flared to a wide base at the bottom. Long, curved handrails ran along the sides, ensuring the safety or any visitors.

The porch was enclosed with clear Plexiglas, which is unique in that Plexiglas is not known for its ventilation qualities. However, this was not a sitting porch; it was a viewing porch, and Mrs. Randolph was known for her ever-changing display.

On expensive wicker furniture, delicately painted to offset the woven strands of rattan, Mrs. Randolph had assembled a rather impressive collection of mannequins, each dressed in period garb. Today we saw three children at play upon the furniture around the porch. One sat at a table and examined some out-of-sight picture or booklet. Another, much younger child, stood and looked off as if following some friends in the distance. The third child was beginning the service of a summer tea for some assumed anticipated guests.

Each mannequin was dressed authentic clothing notable for the perhaps a Victorian type era. They were undoubtedly representative of the height of casual fashion for that time. Pink bows upon white, cotton dresses, straw hats with bands of flowered material, wide dresses with thick underskirts and authentic shoes made the two young girls seem alive. The tea set was delicate in pattern and lovely to look at.

The boy was dressed in three quarter pants which buttoned along the side. His outfit was somewhat reminiscent of a Navy uniform, but having room for running and play. His shoes were genuine vintage of the time being displayed, but appeared somewhat large, as if dress up.

The scene was well planned and crafted to seem natural. The best window displays in posh stores could not quite imitate the look of Mrs. Randolph's array.

Mrs. Randolph was married to one of the community's more prosperous merchants. Mister owned the lumber and hardware store in Randolph which still did a sufficient business among the farmers of the area to remain open and well stocked. He was one of the few fortunate business owners who were still needed.

As a result of his success, she is allowed the hobby of obtaining or making period garments for her life-sized dress up dolls. She takes great pride in her displays, as does all of Randolph, and sets her still life for the enjoyment of all who care to look. Each season brings two or three new scenes to the porch with each one crafted to reflect a holiday or the particular character of the season. Folks often gather to watch her change the scenes, complimenting her fine work. Nothing in Randolph brings more cameras out of cases than Mrs. Randolph's porch.

At night the porch is illuminated by the lights Mister had installed in hidden places along the porch ceiling and floor. They come on as the sun sets so that the light is always like day. Long after the Randolph family retires for bed, the lights accommodate passing viewers with a good look at the ensemble.

Perhaps that is why, late at night, just before the timer meets its turning off point, a casual viewer can glimpse a phenomenon of motion among the mannequins. Their movements are slight, but certainly real - the movement of an arm or taking a step. They may sit or stand. Some have even seen a wave or watched a face, formerly stone-like, crack a smile or change expression. Some claim to have seen the setting go through the full range of motions it is intended to reflect. A tea party may actually occur. A sledding scene may really happen.

Of course, the Randolph's take these reports as the mindless hallucinations of the jealous or spiteful. They hear of their mannequins' activities and laugh at the absurdity of such notions. Why, even Mayor Briss and Chief Clark have claimed to see the mannequins move.

Some in town see nothing. Not because the mannequins don't move, but because they no longer turn their heads to look. Perhaps they have seen something they never want to see again. They look ahead, with grim determination, at the street leading to the town of Randolph proper, and their own homes.

Some say it's a shimmer of reflecting light that creates the illusion of movement. Some might say the house is haunted. Some say even clothing can be haunted by the life forces of their long dead owners.

Mrs. Randolph does not believe in ghosts, so to suggest it to her would be to expect too much of one so jaded to the belief in the supernatural. She would openly scoff and note your ignorance and superstition.

So don't tell her. Don't get on her bad side. You know what you saw. And you can always look on down the road and ignore her blasted porch. At least, you can most of the time.

The Dying Home

Candice sat in the driveway and watched the house through the fogged window of her dilapidated station wagon; a car that did not accurately reflect her financial status. She crushed a cigarillo out in the carved stone ashtray that she had Velcroed to the hump between the seats on the firewall of her car. It was already heaping over with chewed, plastic-tipped butts – room for one more. It had been 17 years since she, or any other Ryan, had sat outside this house and looked in. Moving slowly, she opened the door and pulled the driveway gate open.

She glanced at the sky and the descending sun. Her sports watch glowed 6:56. Starting the engine she glided through the small drive gate and got out to refasten it closed. Still moving slowly, she gathered her few necessary packages on her lap, determining that the rest of the fully packed car could wait until morning. She scanned the midsummer skies over this northeastern Ohio farm lane, with its fields of corn surrounding the house on this side and the expanding housing development across the street still mostly under construction, and wondered again if returning was the right thing. To reclaim her family farm, abandoned by her for nearly two decades, was a decision that surprised everyone she knew, including herself. It probably was linked with the news that she had inoperable cancer and was doomed. She figured she could glean a few months more than the doctors promised, but she knew it was a matter of cellular division and rate of spreading. Real interesting stuff as long as it's in someone else's body.

Candice Ryan was home.

Finally, she drove the short distance to the house and again was caught by the illumination of the setting sun. The bright, clean light was golden and rich upon the white farm with black trim and black roofing. Behind it stood the numerous outbuildings, red with green roofs, looking all the typical style of farms in the know. Everything was newly painted and in order, just as she had arranged from her LA condo. With a nod, she decided that the final check might just include a small bonus of appreciation to Dan of Valley Painting Co. What else could she do with her gazillions?

She walked to the side door, aware that the freshness of the outside would not extend inside the house. Propping the screen door with her hip she searched her cavernous leather bag for her only key to Ryan Manor, as Grandpa used to call it. Frustrated, she returned to the car and fished unsuccessfully in the glove box. A corner of white told her that the envelope holding the key had slipped under the seat.

Retrieving it, she read the logo of the South Russell Legal Partners law firm on the top left corner. She could recite the three pages within by heart. In essence, she was it - the last remaining Ryan to whom all family claims, properties and holdings were due. A list followed with the specifics of the holdings, now hers, and a jolly offer from Mr. Soren Willings to remain at her service should he be needed. A half page was also enclosed noting their fees for management of the estate, filings and various trips to exotic islands with equally exotic girlfriends that she was sure the "miscellaneous" notation really meant. And there was the key to the house, taped to cardboard, with which she could re-enter the homestead of her youth. She shivered as she tore the key from under the tape, dropping the rest of the packet onto the floor. The post date was over seven years old.

Standing again, she surveyed the "back forty" from here. It was hard to believe that this was worth well over a million bucks in real estate. Harder still to comprehend that her various family members all managed to squirrel away an additional $2.6 million in various banks in the area. The real bite was that this tidy sum only reflected about a tenth of her actual worth. Hollywood had been very good to her over these past 17 years. One of the few working leading ladies, turned director, turned producer, with a few writing credits of major hits, she had done very well in the entertainment field. Small town girl makes good and all of that. Just a bit over fifty and now life is all but done.

She sagged as she slipped the key into the lock and turned. She shoved her way into the webbed and dusty mud room/coat room/ basement steps room/book bag room complete with tiny freezer and Grandma's antique radio with the curved top and lighted dial. She had been explicit that all refurbishing be external only, nothing inside was to be disturbed. That was her responsibility.

The place was a mess of mouse droppings, stale air, and moldy carpet. Even the receding sunshine looked dirty as it shoved its way through the long neglected windows. She slid the catch on the screen door, airing the room with some much needed freshness. She placed her bags on the bench just inside the door. Out of habit she hung her light jacket on one of the pegs that Dad had installed along the wall for coats. She crossed the floor and hesitated outside of the kitchen, fighting the rush of memories of what mom called the Ryan Family Nerve Center.

Everything was in perfect order; although there was a haze of accumulated dust that had built up since the last quarterly cleaning arranged by the lawyers of the estate. It was to be expected with no one living there in over 11 years. That was how long it had been since her brother, Seth, the last residing Ryan, committed suicide in the barn. She missed the funeral because no one knew how to reach her. That's how she had planned it. That's why it took those legal eagles years to track her down with news of her inheritance. Almost no one, outside of her family and they were all dead, connected that Candice Ryan, farm girl, and Joanna Leah Rigby, belle of the Hollywood ball for all of these years, were one and the same.

She slowly wandered the downstairs rooms. They were almost exactly had they had been when she lived here as a girl and young woman.

The oak trim and doors. The hardwood maple floors. Bookshelves in the family room laden with classics. The dinner table which seated 12 that grandpa had brought with him from Poland. All was intact and resting under that sheen of soft dust. Absently she ran a finger across the table, tracing the grain of the wood and leaving a furrow not unlike those among the rows of corn outside her windows.

She tied her hair back with a Scrunch and unbuttoned her shirt, hanging it on the back of the master chair at the head of the table. Her watch noted to her that she had about six minutes. Quickly she began pulling back the yellowed curtains that hung closed in all the downstairs windows in the front of the house. There was so much life to yet see. She wanted to capture as much of the setting sunshine as she could pack into these front rooms. Looking around, she was mildly lifted in spirit.

What Candice did not see was the apparition of a young boy, about seven or so, who appeared behind her as she opened the curtain over the picture window. He had emerged from nowhere and stood watching her in the archway between the family room and music room. Candice did not see him. The curtains were crumbling, as old sun rotted cotton will, making it difficult to slide them to the sides. With a tear and a shove, they moved aside spilling light from the orange sun into the room; fading the young, still boy to a dim outline. With a glance to him, Candice returned to the kitchen.

Over the next two hours, she turned the kitchen around. The non-functioning chamber was up and running. Appliances were plugged back in and humming. The clock was set and all of the surfaces got a wiping or mopping. Although the musty, dense smells of being too-long-closed were still evident, they now played second scent to pine cleaner and polish. Satisfied and exhausted, Candice pulled a chair out and sat in front of the kitchen door. It was nearly 9:30 now and she didn't want to miss her Pa coming home from the barns.

Hands on her lap she fixed her gaze on the main barn that stood about 50 yards from the house. Pa made his appearance just beyond the small man door that was cut into the huge main sliding barn door. He had put that in himself and was proud of it. Why open the whole big pig of a barn door when you could pass through a regular door with no effort. Neither door opened this night, but Pa came home just the same; face one big smile, Cleveland Indians cap tilted to one side of his head, hair spilling out in all directions. He looked up, as he did every night at this time, and waved. His bib overalls were dirty and torn in one knee and his zipper was down as it had been since his first appearance 22 years ago. You'd think that, if nothing else, he'd find a way to get that zipper back up to where it's supposed to be. Tears filled her eyes. He looked so good under the barn lights.

Pa faded just before the back door. For a moment, she thought he might just make it home this time. She still distinctly remembered the day that this walk between barn and house actually occurred. She and Pa had gone fishing down at Paw Paw Lake, less than a mile from home. They went most Tuesdays in the summer, just the two of them, catching their limit and always throwing them back in for next week. He had taken his final walk through the barns to check on animals and equipment, as he did every night before removing his shoes the final time, and was heading in to catch the game on their old black and white. The first time it happened, the original time, she had seen him coming and thrown open the door, extending to him a big glass of unsweetened lemonade that she had just fresh squeezed. Pa like it filled with sugar so she was setting him up for a big trick. Not a grain of sugar had been spooned into the large, frosty tumbler. He had taken a big swig, his face alight with delight both in his drink and his daughter, swallowing contentedly. When he finally tasted the sour beverage, he squealed and chased her, both laughing, out around the house. It was a good memory. Pa died less than a week later when his tractor overturned somehow and crushed him. Sighing, she whispered that she'd see him later and closed the screen door to the night insects.

In time she had the family room under control and was ready to sleep. She grabbed her night bag from the car after parking it in the garage around back of the house, closing the doors. She decided to take a look upstairs in the morning and made up a bed of the couch. She slept with the TV and kitchen lights on. It would take a while before she would be comfortable again at home.

Throughout the night, ghostly figures moved through the house attending to chores or heading someplace long forgotten. Candice slept through the night leaving the occupants unattended and alone. Only one, her grandpa, noticed she was there, sleeping on the couch. He watched for a time and, as he faded, cleared his throat loudly. Candice heard nothing.

In her dreams, she again revisited many of the places which delighted her as a girl. She swam with friends at Paw Paw. Rode her bike into town to have a milkshake at Lincoln's Lunch Counter. Two teachers entered her dreamed memories. Mr. Blick, from whom she received her first and only paddling; a "whack" as the kids called it, and Mr. Stonehauser, for whom she held her first "crush." Other remembrances flowed as the night moved toward dawn: her first Beatles album, the time Tommy Spitzer tried to kiss her, fireworks at the park, the Memorial Day walk to the cemetery, Squaw Rock and cigarettes, and her passion to be a great Hollywood actress.

She awoke with her familiar hacking cough. Cigars are rough on the throat. She made coffee and decided, just like that, not to smoke another one for the rest of her too likely, too short life. With uneasiness, she decided to eat breakfast in town at the Colonial Diner. Finally being home, it was somewhat difficult to leave Ryan Manor. But starvation wins out every time.

Entering the iconic Chagrin Falls eatery, she flashed on how unpresentable she must be. *Maybe it will work in my favor and no one will notice me.* It was the slow zone between the breakfast wait list and the lunch crush.

"Sit where you want, hon." Called the tall server wiping down the worn Formica of the counter. She paused in her buffing circles and watched Candice amble over to small two-top against the wall.

Candice knew the look and curled up in fetal position inside. The young woman plucked a menu from the rack and opened it, handing it to Candice.

"Coffee?" the Server offered.

Turning over her mug, Candice nodded, shielding her face with her menu.

As she poured, the savvy waitress leaned in and in a low voice said, "You are just another diner today, Miss Rigby. You get no swooning from me." Topping off the steaming coffee she said, "The window table just opened and it is the most invisible spot in the place. Let's move you over there before the early lunchers come in."

Without waiting for a response, the girl picked up Candice's mug and walked her to the table she had recommended. Putting the mug on the table she pulled out the chair at the corner seat. As Candice sat, noting that most of the restaurant was obscured from this cubby, she locked eyes and said, "I won't forget this in the tip."

Laughing, the waitress, who had *Eryn* stitched in her diner shirt, returned with a wink, "The customary percent is fine. None of this $9.25 breakfast and dropping a tenner. Deal?"

Sipping her still molten coffee, Candice thought to herself, *I guess I am home.*

After eggs and potatoes as only the Colonial could make them (she imagined that they mixed in a pinch of Small Town America for the special taste of home), she turned into the office of Ronald Hannick, a local handyman and properties maintenance agent, to thank and pay him for getting her power, gas and phone turned on. She regretted that she did not think to have him hire a cleaning service for the inside.

"Ms. Ryan," protested Ron, "this is way too much money."

In small town style, he tried to refuse the generous bonus she included for him, taking it only after she assured him how much he aided her.

"Don't be ungrateful," Candice snapped with more edge than she had meant. "How was I ever going to arrive in a place that is livable if not for your efforts?" Today was turning into Tip Tuesday. Settling down a bit, she decided to explore some other needs with Ronald.

"Mr. Hannick, would you be willing and interested in attending to some additional work around the farm? And maybe taking care of the mowing and weeding?"

"Ummm," Ron hesitated. "Lawn stuff isn't really my line of work. But I'll be most happy to keep some work going on your buildings if you need. I have lots lined up for the summer, but if you aren't in a rush, your place would be the perfect kind of work to keep my guys busy between jobs."

"That would be fine," said Candice with relief. "And here's what we can do. I'll have you buy me a riding lawn mower for the farm, and I'll contract with you for the grass cutting and attention to the gardens. I pay you and you pay some responsible kid. And I know it's silly, but I'd prefer a girl if you can manage to find one. It's how I made my summer money as a girl and I always felt so good about a regular mowing job. Only boys got those jobs and it would delight me to no end to see a girl continuing what I started."

Candice knew this all sounded stupid, but it was those hours on the mower, free from distraction and dialogue, that were so key to her figuring out what she wanted in and from life.

"And Mr. Hannick, also buy an extra gas can and a pair of over the ear protective thingies." At this she cupped her ears like ear muffs. "And a weed whip."

"Will do, Miss Ryan," said Ron, jotting this all down in his permanent pocket notebook. Fleetingly he thought he might ask for her autograph, but he intuitively speculated that this would be seen as a personal affront.

Quite surprised at how comfortable it all felt, she left Ronald to gather food from the market. Strangely, it was beginning to feel quite good being back in Chagrin. Maybe she could maintain her hope of some obscurity.

Skipping lunch, Candice put away her groceries and headed for the upstairs of her house. Initially she was excited to see the old rooms but as she placed her foot on the first step, she froze in the memory of why she had left her family behind in the first place. Slowly looking up, she saw her mother, not a ghost, but as a vivid and almost alive memory, glaring down at her and screaming that she was a slut and demon child. She took off her shoe and threw it at her daughter, following it with the other one. Both missed her but made a mark in her soul that all of the years in between could not erase or heal. Candice knew it was not unforgiveness. It was sadness.

After Pa died, her mother had "slipped" a bit mentally and was always seeing sexual promiscuity in the lives and actions of her children. Candice couldn't speak for her two older brothers, but she knew that she was one of half a dozen girls who made it through high school with her virginity intact. Of course, college in the 70's held little chance for her to retain that esteemed status very long once she left home, but lasting through high school was worth something. Being slightly sexually active was not grounds for sluthood. Too bad mom found the two condoms she had brought home with her from Kent State University.

The ensuing fight was both violent and discourteous. Mom dredged up every instance in which Candice had not lived to her measure. Candice, being hard headed, decided not to take it. Packing her car after mom had predictably sedated herself with a valium; she stole a road map from her brother's car and headed west to stardom. Of course, no one believed that she would or could ever make it. But she did.

She was "discovered" through a call for extras for a sitcom. It bombed, being ill conceived and mundane, but she was noticed, mostly for her body and hair, and received a call for an hour long detective show which was to star heartthrob Robert James Morgan. She got the role of the buxom mechanic Char, who always had an investigative tip and a smile for Mr. Morgan, a.k.a. Matty Duke, which was the name of the popular series. Her single season was shortened when her part was written out and she was "killed" for assisting Duke in a case. A la 70's TV, she was crushed while working on Duke's car by thugs who hit the drop button on the car jack she was working under. But now her foot was in the door and other parts came her way. She actually did quite well and received her big break when she and a half dozen other Hollywood punks got cast in a sleeper movie about the way young people lived after disco. After an agonizingly slow start, it reached cult status among those her age around the country, and eventually became a mega-hit. Other roles followed and she continually received accolades from critics and movie-goers alike. Eventually, she attained a level of stardom usually reserved for males. She became one of an elite corps of women who held Hollywood by the proverbial short hairs. It was a great run for a farm girl and she never looked back.

Her mom died accidentally in a car wreck. The Lake Erie Snow Belt was delivering one of its historic white-out burials. Mom had visited friends near Ravenna, well out of the Snow Belt, and returned home too late for good sense. A plow truck hit her head on only a mile from home, killing her immediately. Although she sent flowers in her real name, she could not drop her anger and return home. Other spirits, visible and invisible, barred her from being able to ever return again. At least that's what she thought prior to becoming ill.

Shaking her head to clear the cobwebs of these recollections, she faced her fears and ascended to the floor above. She explored the rooms with teary-eyed wonder, caught in memories of delight and marvel. Her room, although changed to accommodate guests, still was recognizable and filled with her essence. So were her parent's room, and the room where grandpa slept until his death in a hunting accident. Kurt, her brother who had been killed in Viet Nam, shared a room at the end of the hall with Seth, the one killed by his own hand. Their bunk beds were draped with sheets, resembling a large, square coffin of white. Apparently, Seth, the last Ryan resident, had slept somewhere else.

Cleaning the upstairs rooms she would use - her bedroom, the larger bathroom, and the sewing room - took her most of the day. At times, her attentions were diverted as a shape or specter floated through the hall or a shadow flitted across a window. She did her best to ignore them but each occurrence reminded her of the other side of life on Ryan Farm. It was a shared life with the dead, or at least the part of the dead that most would call ghosts. Her tasks completed, she returned to the kitchen to fix a frozen chicken pot pie and a salad, a far cry from her evenings in California at divine restaurants of world fame.

Following her meal, she began unpacking her car. It was now approaching 24 hours after her arrival and she was aware that an appointment to keep. By 6:30, she was planted in the living room, picture window at her back and grandpa's rocker directly before her. He would join her shortly for one of his "heart-to-hearts." Absently she ran her hand through her hair to assure that she was presentable. She had yet to bathe, but thought all else was satisfactory. Grandpa was old world and expected that his family be appropriate for family time. This meant that no one looked as though they just came in from barn or field and just plopped down. Even though that had always been exactly the case for this family farm, grandpa maintained that a rinsing and a change of clothes was all it took to enter civility and graceful living. Over the years, Candice found that his transplanted Polish values made sense.

A second before he appeared his chair rocked slightly. And then he was there.

"So you have returned home, Candice." he said with his thick eastern European accent. Only he could be counted on to call her by her given name. She hated Candy.

"I am home, Grandpa. I've come back to die. I have cancer." She whispered.

They sat in silence for a long time. Candice was uncertain if she should speak or even if she could. Grandpa nodded. His caterpillar shaped, gray eyebrow rose in prelude to his sentence.

"Ahh. The cancer. I have expected you for some time. I am at sorrow to receive you home with this news. Will you die soon? You do not look so near death."

"I…I don't know. The doctors say soon but I don't feel it. It's in there, though, Grandpa. I'm full of it." Her head fell into her hand. Her temples ached.

"We will talk more, Candice. I accept you back into our home. We will live together in peace." He faded and was gone. She sat and watched his chair as it ceased its rocking.

Later that evening the young boy returned in the archway. This time Candice smiled at him, uncertainly, and spoke his name. It was Charlie, the first ghost to inhabit the farm. He was her oldest brother, born and died in his bed years before she was conceived. A fever took him after he had fought off pneumonia and a bronchial infection. A plain, garden variety fever that burned his exhausted body and cooked his brain. No one expected him to die but it was the final "too much." Mom found him dead in his bed when she got up to give him more fluids and some aspirin. His nightly haunting began after his burial.

Candice watched him until he vanished, as she had all her life. He never acknowledged her; he never had. His was a visitation without awareness or energy to move. He simply came and left.

As the days of mid-summer shifted to late summer, Candice spent time with each of the visitations. As a girl she had noted the times and places and visitors on the wall inside her closet, above her closet door. In small printing she had made her log of the ghostly activities which were an unchanging part of this house of family spirits. Without looking, she knew it was still there, unpainted after all these years.

Grandma walked through the upstairs halls at different times each night. In her final years, she never left the floor. She was too infirm to use the stairs. In her spirit-self she was still quite weak, dragging herself in a painful shuffle from room to room. Only during her last nightly appearance was she ever able to nod in recognition and pass a word or a smile. She was always calling Candice her "Sweet Candy." Candice often wondered how she knew it was her after all these years. But Grandma knew.

Seth's appearances surprised Candice. He died long after she had left Ryan Manor so his visitations were new to her. As she learned his patterns, she noted them with the others in her closet, dragging her desk chair into the closet as she did when she was younger. Even the pencil remained where she last placed it in the crack between the wall and the door trim. Inscribed on the trusty #2 pencil was CANDICE RYAN CHAGRIN SCHOOLS as if it was all her proper, full name. It was a gift from her elementary school principal. She gave them to all her students advancing to the Middle School. She could not remember her name but she clearly recalled her exotic cat eyed glasses frames and constant, loud nasal sniff. Her fingers traced the bite marks she left in the orange and black paint surface those long years ago.

Seth had hung himself in the back barn by throwing a rope over the beam of the hayloft and jumping from a tractor wheel. She knew that he choked to death and didn't snap his neck as she knew he would have hoped. He was the weakest Ryan and not one for pain or discomfort. Sadly, she remembered her closest brother and his eternally melancholy eyes.

Those eyes met hers again as she was brushing her teeth in the kitchen sink one evening soon after she returned home. She had wondered if Seth had "appearing times" as the family had always called these supernatural showings. Now she knew she had been looking in the wrong place. His time was 10:35pm and out in the garden area that had added so much color to summers. It was rather barren now, having not been planted for at least a decade.

He wandered the garden observing plants no longer there. Just before fading he turned to the house and approached the kitchen window, a large double hung over the sinks, and waved. He had been so young and healthy, so full of life. Now his life was colorless and translucent.

Seth was the Ryan who had made most of the fortune she inherited. He was a shrewd business man and wise investor. His dealings in real estate development had netted him a considerable sum over the years. His profits went directly into the emerging computer markets and he reaped dividends beyond anyone's speculations - even his own. And yet, with all of his money he could not replace his family. Although a note was never found explaining why, she knew in her heart that he took his own life to be with the family once again.

Why Ryan Farm kept its dead was never known to family members. It just did. However, only those who died there, stayed there. Kurt, shot in Viet Nam and buried in the township cemetery, never made a return trip home. Neither did her mother who perished only a mile down the road. Yet it was a mile too far for her to make the trip back. Pa, grandma and grandpa, Seth, and little Charlie made their daily tours throughout the house and yard at the same time each day.

By the end of August, the cancer was making itself known throughout her body. The mirror began showing her how it was consuming her, reducing skin tone and luster to a sagging gray. Energy reserves began to be expended. Her joints hurt and it stung to urinate. She began to realize things could go quickly. Flashes of pain sometimes shot through her insides. Her appetite declined, as did her stamina. She vowed not to seek medical assistance to make her "comfortable," whatever that was supposed to mean. Eryn, her favorite waitress at the Colonial, couldn't hold back a comment asking Candice if that was anything she could do.

Were it not for her daily visits with Grandpa she would have despaired and perhaps followed Seth's lead.

"Did I ever tell you about how Charlie used to love to walk and watch his feet?" asked Grandpa one evening. "He would go back and forth, up that driveway to the road, and turn around again, time after time, never taking his eyes off of his feet."

"What was he looking at?" Candice asked?

"Never knew. He'd just pace and kick some gravel and watch his feet take steps. One time he walked on by me as I was sitting with a lemonade Gramma made me and he looked up at me, never missing a step, and said 'My feet...they walk.'"

Both Ryans laughed even as grandpa faded for another evening.

Candice was never sure how Grandpa could know things, but he had knowledge of life from after his time on earth. One evening he weighed in on his opinions about the state of the planet, and one a different occasion he wanted to know what Candice thought of the rapid pace of advancing technology.

But most reoccurring was how Grandpa encouraged her to focus on what time she had left. They conversed about life in the past, revisiting stories and fun times, reliving holidays and special "blow ups" of family anger that had become legendary. Both knew it was all part of family.

As fall began to slowly fade into winter, Candice grasped that she, too, was fading into the winter of her demise. She had to finish her distribution of riches to the people and organizations she deemed worthy of her gifts. To avoid any snags, she enlisted, as other family members had, the services of the South Russell Legal Partners. The partner she selected was a compassionate woman named Margaret who treated her respectfully and did not fawn over her stardom. Instead, she gushed about the things Candice embraced as important, like the farm.

In early winter Grandpa spoke to her about preparing for her death. This was not an off limits subject for her. She was strong enough to speak of what was inevitable, but she noted something strange in Grandpa's tone.

"Your death, Candice. What are your thoughts?" Grandpa asked with an unwavering eye.

"I am ready to go, Grandpa. I am way too young to die, but now I'm far too consumed by this hateful disease to live much longer."

"My dear," he began with sympathy filling his colorless, clear eyes, "to live here you cannot just die. Your life must be taken and it must be taken here. You have returned home so you'll satisfy that part of whatever lets us live on. But you must die in a taking of your life, not slipping into death by death's means."

"I don't understand." Candice said with a note of confusion. She began shredding the tissue she held on her lap.

"Your father was taken by the tractor. Seth by his own hands. It is not just the death, but the kind of death that lets you remain."

"But you and Grammy and Charlie," she began, stammering, "you all just died and I can see you here."

"Your grandmother, may God eternally bless her, died falling down the steps. The steps took her. I was killed by the bullet of another hunter as I returned home across our fields shooting a few geese in our back corn fields. It was stray; a missed shot I suppose. The idiot likely never knew he hit me. See how it works. A durn citified rube claimed me on our land." Candice was silent, barely breathing as Grandpa filled in so many gaps. Finally, she stirred.

"But I see Charlie every day. I've seen him my whole life. He died of fever. That's not different from my dying from cancer." She felt the urge to vomit suddenly. Sweat glistened on her face.

"You have never been told but Charlie was killed by your parents in a terrible accident. Your Papa gave him his medicine and went to do the milking. Soon after your mother also gave him his medicines. He was accidentally poisoned by the two who loved him the most." Grandpa looked sadder than any creature she had ever seen.

"How horrible," she whispered.

"The doctor told me this. We never told your parents for it would have killed them. They both died blaming the fevers. It met no purpose to tell them what they did."

They sat in silence and Grandpa's head drooped forward in sadness as he faded from sight. She wondered if he could still see her or if she seemed to fade to him, also. He never answered her inquiries about his life beyond death.

Too puzzled to do more, she retired to her bed. For long hours she stared at the black motes of imagined light which lingered and floated along the ceiling, thinking, puzzling about what she was learning of life in this home.

Over the following days, Candice and Grandpa talked more of her death. Grandpa had a plan but Candice was unconvinced.

Ronald Hannick was called to the farm for long hours in the weeks following. Bits of her decisions were shared with him. She had decided to remain on the farm until death and he would be key in making that death successful. If he could believe. Mr. Hannick had become a great support to her emotionally and in his capacity as a properties manager. He had met all of her needs and even found a delightful teenaged girl to mow and trim the weeds. She wanted this to become his house in the near future. After many discussions, and a few shocking and reality-changing visual revelations that expanded his understanding of the cosmos and life, Mr. Hannick consented to become a partner in self-determination. A final draft of her will was sent to her lawyer. By the New Year she was ready.

In her final days, Candice prayed more than at any time before in her life. It was not a reckoning with God, but a careful consideration of loose ends she could never finishing tying. She became thankful and actually felt a sense of letting go, as a trapeze artist must do in order to have hands free for the next swinging bar which will propel to new places.

She also walked the farm, in a slow, shivering, hobble, to see it again for the last time. Her final tour was revisited each day until she was truly ready.

Days into the New Year she recorded in multiple diaries all she knew of the farm, the family, and her life. She confessed and recorded in her "Dear Ronald" who she really was as a person, a family member and as an actor, in a conversational style. Ronald would be the carrier of the story. It was easier for her to record all of this as an extremely long letter with a specific recipient in mind.

As mid-January approached, on a dark, snowy Friday evening, she dialed 9-1-1 to report an attempted break-in. A painted brick, which would later release finger prints matching hers, was heaved through the front door window. Her frantic and fearful cries, recorded forever on slow moving police bias tape for the eternal confounding of the local constabulary, would plead for quick action and intervention. She feared her life might be lost and she was oh-so-ill. The burglar was coming, coming… and the line went dead.

From the destroyed window, she could hear the responding units approaching. Making the sign of the cross and kissing both the Star of David and the Crucifix of Jesus dangling between her breasts, she picked up the old shotgun and pressed her back against the wall next to the now open door. As the red and blue lights washed the house with carnival brilliance, she watched as Grandpa appeared right on time. She threw him a thumbs-up, not entirely sure he understood the gesture, and smiled a knowing smile. He nodded back and saluted. *So like him,* she thought.

The echoes of running boots were filling her air, doors were slamming, and guns cocked into firing positions. A flurry of questions and commands came to her amidst the falling snow. They were close enough.

She ran into the night, gun brandished high and pointing out, with a scream of terror. She barely felt the rounds that filled her body and took the dimming flames of her life. She recognized the voice of Officer Ramsey as he yelled for the others to hold fire. At least someone still recognized her in spite of the wasting that cancer had reckoned in her. With no more thought, Candice Ryan died on her farm, her life taken by others.

In the spring, Ron moved in. He'd visited many times and at all hours. For his part in assuring the Ryan family had a home forever, he would never be required to work again. Just the same, he needed to make sure that the "ghosties," as he called them, were as accepting of him as he was of them.

He liked Grandpa plenty because he could talk, and would talk from time to time. The others were just no problem and by early summer, it was like watching for a bird to return to the barns or ponds, as some do each year to nest and lay eggs.

Candice looked good, too. She made three appearances a day. Twice in the evenings among the fields and out buildings, looking satisfied and full of the strange death-living of ghosts. Each midnight she would drift from the bathroom to her bedroom, clothed in glory, ready for a good night's sleep.

And every night she would wish him sweet dreams.

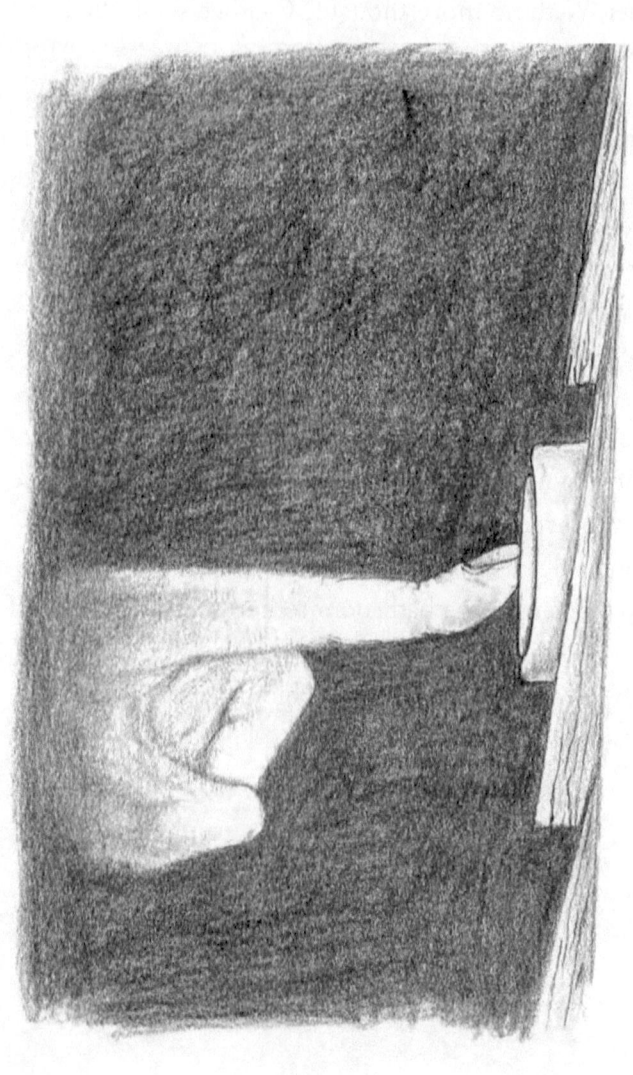

The Nicest Girl You've Ever Met

L ittle Angel Kelley would be gravely missed. So thought the entire
Paw Paw Lake community, and they were right, for Angel was
an aptly named reflection of her character and personality. Intuitively
she knew how to treat folks just right and without manipulation. And
although she was only 13 years old, Angel was the perfect child and
neighbor. She openly loved everyone and everyone on Paw Paw simply
loved her.

Paw Paw Lake is a conscientiously progressive development
which, through the wisdom of its designers and residents, gently and
tastefully wrapped its homes around the lake with respect to nature.
Among the numerous lake communities of northern Ohio, Paw Paw
Lake was a startling example of how people and nature could live in
mutual support and cooperation.

This design layout seemed to permeate the residents of Paw Paw
Lake, giving them a special grace for one another. People felt attached
to the community and resisted leaving. In fact, they more often than
not tended to live their lives right here on Paw Paw. If not born on the
lake, they would join the community with that original purchase and
remain until that certain movement to the grave. A number of the 45
or so homes still boasted possession into the second generation. And
some in the next generation, the third since forest and lake were con-
verted into residential development, would very likely continue the
custom of family possession. Such was the magnetic quality of life in
this pristine communal fellowship.

Angel's family was one of the fortunate newcomers who came
across the house on the day it was initially listed with a realtor. Elderly
Earl Barnett, a World War I veteran and agent for the county extension

agency in agriculture, died in the home of good and natural causes. Never marrying, his estate was turned over to the Congregational Church in Chagrin in a windfall that surprised even the oldest member of that fine congregation. Old timers knew Earl and they also knew that good Mr. Barnett only visited annually for the Christmas Candlelight service. They also knew that he never contributed when the offering was collected. Yet, his will left everything to the church. The reasons for why the bequest was made were never known. An act of gratitude? Perhaps a kindness returned? The intention died with old Mr. Barnett. The basis for his largesse was never accurately speculated.

The minister of the Chagrin Congregational Church, the Reverend Andre' Kloppers, gave his wife Alison the task of selling the house. Mrs. Kloppers was an agent for the Chagrin Valley Realty Company. Cries of objections on grounds of Conflict of Interest were never raised – even by those who deemed it certainly was such. Obviously, Mrs. Kloppers would receive no more than she earned on a straight commission. But some raised their eyebrows nonetheless. Inappropriate or not, there was no one in the church likely to challenge the decision – Alison Kloppers was not a woman to contest or clash sabers with.

Weeks later, after the will cleared Probate Court, Mrs. Kloppers listed the home routinely in the AM and found herself showing it in the PM. She led Patrick and Becky Kelley through the house which Patrick described as being "the gleam of angelic wings with God's most favorable intentions." While Mrs. Kloppers had no ear for this Irish phrase (which turned out to be Mr. Kelley's own working and nothing traditionally Irish), she did note the religious nature of Mr. Kelley's exclamation and proceeded to think she would get two commissions in one sale. A house sold and a new family in church. She was only mildly disappointed to learn the Kelley family was devoutly Catholic and not very good evangelism prospects. She'd get the house commission either way. And the Trustees would be delighted with the quick sale of this extremely valuable property.

Contented with their great fortune and the house of their dreams, the Kelley's prosperity grew in their first year as residents of Paw Paw Lake. Mrs. Kelley was promptly hired at the Chagrin Library as assistant librarian; Mr. Kelley as head pharmacist at Valley Drug. But both found total elation when Mrs. Kelley killed the proverbial rabbit under the care of young Dr. Duffield. Married for nearly twenty years and still childless, the Kelleys held no hope for pregnancy. Tampering with the Almighty's wisdom and will was not to be presumed upon by modern medicine. Mr. Kelley believed it to be "the water" of their new community, which followed the same logic his mother used when asked to explain where his little sister had come from.

Angel Marie Robin Kelley was born in the fall as Bill Haley and his Comets counted the hours of the newly born Rock and Roll clock. This clock would not tick long for Angel, barely introducing her to the British Invasion.

In her short life, Angel was a blessing to all who knew her. As a child, she glowed, causing the crankiest stranger to pause in reflection of the preciousness of youth. In elementary school, she was everyone's best friend and the favorite student of every teacher she ever had. Her Brownie troop always benefited during the annual cookie sale from her presence and involvement. Church school teachers saw her as the perfect example of how Jesus would have been had he been born female. In middle school, she was a model student. Baby-sitting jobs became nearly a career, the demand for her services being so great. All the boys loved her in her budding pre-adolescence and no adult could find fault in her. She had no secret sins, no perverse longings, no guile or malice of heart. She was a human example of the qualities of love and kindness in their purest forms.

Yet, her mortality was imminent.

Angel knew each and every community member of Paw Paw Lake well. Frequently she would slowly meander from house to house, door to door, to seek a neighbor's support for some school, scouting, church, or community need. No matter the plea, Angel was never re-fused, nor were any disturbed at her multi-annual visits with coin box or sales catalogue in hand. She was always the top seller or charitable funds collector. Even angry old widow Cirello, the nasty Italian lady who chased the neighbor kids, dogs and paperboys from her yard with a broom, would be seen turning her broom around, in its proper posi-tion, and sweeping her walk in anticipation of Angel's visit, no matter what the cause.

Once she was overheard calling across to Angel as Angel complet-ed a cookie order at the Thomas home. "Angel! Angel, my love! You no-a forgetta to come' n' see Nana?"

Angel called back with a wave, "How could I ever forget you Mrs. Cirello? You're my favorite stop. That's why I save you for last, so I can visit you longer."

As Mrs. Cirello broke into a glorious and seldom seen smile, Angel whispered to Mrs. Thomas something about the importance of honoring our elderly for their investment into our lives and communi-ties. Mrs. Thomas, in her own heart, could find no investment that the wretched widow had ever placed anywhere. Angel bounded away to the freshly swept walk of Mrs. Cirello.

And so, life passed for Angel. Short life that it was.

No violence befell Angel. Her goodness makes one suspect that her untimely demise might be from the hand of someone evil, in an attempt to sway the balance of heavenly forces in eternal battle. No murderer or rapist killed her. No drunk driver or speeding teenager. Not even a disease or bee sting. Her life simply stopped in her sleep a mere six days after her 13th birthday.

Aging Dr. Corrigan, the county coroner and friend of Mr. Kelley through the pharmacy, ruled it death by natural causes, sighting some obscure study examining the weakening heart valves of adolescent girls. In truth, there was no such study and he never examined her in-ternally. The good doctor found it impossible to mar the natural beauty of this young divine so suited to her very name. Only God knew that Corrigan's guess was inaccurate and that Angel had fallen victim to a brain aneurysm in her sleep on that staggering night. She died so quickly that imagining minds could argue effectively that Angel likely never knew she was dead.

Such arguments would not be untrue.

Never had a death drawn such a response. Angel's calling hours, funeral, and memorial services seemed to draw more mourners than the death of former president James Garfield, a one-time resident of these same valleys and hills. It seemed as though the entire valley area had turned out. And, in truth, it had. The community, both secular and sacred, had taken Angel's passing as personally as if she were one of their own.

The Kelleys grieved hard and long. Their miracle was now gone. But oh, the memories - vacations and campfires, Christmas decorating and back-to-school shopping, they wrapped themselves in the cocoon of silent reminiscence. School plays and Children's Choir performances were remembered. Her kind words, her thoughts shared, her smile - all were now the vestiges of a world found only in heart and mind. Both cried often - alone and together.

For the residents of Paw Paw, time did what it does so well. It passed on to other attention grabbers such as the proposed road widening project, hearings for the community sewer plans, and the building of a playground at Gurney School. Both Kelleys returned to their professions for some distraction, markedly diminished as the people they had been while Angel lived.

The community rebounded as summer came and went. Swimming and picnics and out-of-town visitors vied for focus. Mrs. Cirello had a fall on July 4th trying to hurry to her phone to get the police to round up the hooligans who were setting off those fireworks down at the lake. From her stay at the hospital after the surgery to rebuild her broken hip, she was transferred to a Catholic nursing home for rehabilitation and healing. She never returned home, dying within the year. A family moved in as Mrs. Cirello moved out. Yards needed mowing, plants were pruned, dogs were walked and somehow, magically, Angel's death became somewhat dim.

In late fall, in the week before what would have been Angel's fourteenth birthday, Mr. Nichols answered their ringing doorbell. So did the Horners and the Bourisseaus and every other resident on Paw Paw Lake. None knew that each bell had rung at precisely the same moment. Only the Kelleys' and the Wangs' bells were silent. The Wangs' bell was broken and thus, inoperable. Their bell button, however, did move inwardly as if pushed by an invisible finger. The Kelleys' bell had been completely undisturbed.

In some homes, no human ears heard the appeal of their doorbells. A few dogs barked, and a cat or two twitched their ears with annoyance. In one home, the Chestons', which was the last house on Paw Paw, two high school hoodlums were attempting to force the back door lock in search of merchandise which they hoped to convert into beer, quickly fled the scene at the sound of the bell.

Along Branch Street, young Suzie Steines noticed that her neighbors, one on each side and the two across the street, all opened their doors at the same time that she had. She felt a chill and quickly shut the darkening evening from her home, returning to homework.

The next evening, at a later hour, each and every front door on each and every Paw Paw Lake residence was knocked sharply five times by an unseen hand. Those answering numbered the majority of the community. Only those away or otherwise occupied, as Renata Krandall was in her vacuuming and Jamil Watson was with a risqué 8mm film he'd received from his college brother, did not answer the door. All the others went to the door to be greeted by no one and turned away with a grumble or a shrug. This time Suzie let her older brother, Ian heed the knock. She suddenly remembered something urgent in her bedroom needing her immediate attention.

Each remaining evening that week, each house on Paw Paw Lake received a similar calling of the occupants to the door. Doors were knocked, doorbells were pressed, or, as on two of the evenings, the front picture windows were tapped feverishly, sending a simultaneous notice to the households. It all stopped on November 2nd, Angel's birthday.

Up to the birthday, puzzling and fearful thoughts were working through the minds of the Paw Paw residents, but nothing was ever spoken. As that week progressed, the community air was beginning to taste lightly of something resembling fear. When November 2nd came and went with no further incident, as did the days following, the collective consciousness of Paw Paw Lake forgot its brush with dread. Even Suzie, whose fears overshadowed all because of what she had noticed, forgot the occurrences in the promise of the upcoming holidays.

The year passed quickly for the Kelleys. Although still morose and somber at the loss of their Angel, they bravely allowed life to continue as normally as it could. Yet, each night, quite unknown to the other, both Patrick and Becky dreamed of Angel. In their sleep, they cried or smiled, sleep closed eyes aglow at seeing her. She was always coming to them with arms open and hungry for their affections. Always coming into their house or car or place of work, in varying clothing and in differing seasons. Always coming and always with a look of delight. Always approaching and exclaiming she would be there soon. It was in these dreams that the Kelleys found their ration of endurance which allowed them to survive another day.

Slowly the months pass, moving through the holidays, into deep winter, then the spring budding of crocuses and summer sunsets and mosquitoes. Finally, October comes again to Paw Paw Lake, as it always does, with a readiness for the fall season in each home. Colored maples and browning oaks inspire the inhabitants. Corn stalks, dried and picked clean of their ears of corn which is saved for winter feed for the animals, are tied to porch posts. Carved pumpkins complete the front door scenes. Storm windows are hung. Lawns mowed a final time between the gathering and burning of leaves. Neighbors stop in their evening walks and talk high school football or children's costumes for Beggar's Night. And, on this second anniversary of Angel's death, they intentionally avoid speaking of the one commonly experienced and troubling event. Once again there is a ringing of doorbells and vacant knocking at front doors.

Remarkably, only Suzie confirms the far reaching nature of the disturbances. Although she refuses to open her door, she peeks through her bedroom curtains and watches as porch lights come on and door after door is opened along her street.

While none actually knew, Angel had returned.

In their quiet home, the Kelleys were experiencing a different phenomenon as their neighbors ignored or answered their doors. This year slight changes were noticed but not discussed.

Angel's room was now a guest room; her bed, dresser, and desk remained. Her regular clothes were sent to the church ministry for the poor. Her special outfits, things like her confirmation dress, her school jacket, her favorite dress, and the flannel nightgown she had sewn in Home Economics — were stored in a box in the attic marked "Angel's Belongings." It was as if Angel were in college and someday to return.

Within her old room, Angel-like occurrences were observed.

The first night of the community door bell ringing, it was noticed that the door of Angel's room was ajar about four inches, just as Angel used to keep it slightly ajar each night when she went to bed. The Kelleys kept it completely open now. Always.

The next night, the light in her bathroom was on and noticed by Mr. Kelley as he made his nightly trip to the kitchen for his stomach medicine.

The next night, nimble walking was heard by Mrs. Kelley, who had lately become a very light sleeper.

On the following night, both noticed that Angel's old bed, now adorned with a southwest Navajo style blanket, which replaced her beloved Raggedy Ann and Andy bed cover, had been turned down. Silently, avoiding her husband's stare, Mrs. Kelley straightened the cover back up and over the pillow.

In the morning, she tucked it in again.

The two remaining nights before what would have been Angel's fifteenth, the Kelleys heard the hangers in Angel's closet rattling against each other. Not in supernatural malignancy, but quietly swaying, as if bumped by a blouse being re-hung. Late the next night, a toilet was flushed.

Deep in that evening before the birthday that wasn't going to be celebrated, in the stillness of their dreams, each of the Kelleys murmured into the night's darkness a greeting to Angel followed by an acknowledgment that she was again at home. Neither heard the confession of the other.

Mr. Kelley went to work the next morning as usual. After he was gone, Mrs. Kelley called in sick. She simply had too much to do on this day to spend time working for others. Why, an entire birthday party doesn't just happen. Even a party for three requires special, focused attention to make everything just so.

As she shopped for Angel's favorite meal of pepper steak and rice with red and green peppers, and her favorite cake, which was German chocolate, "handmade" from a boxed mix, folks noticed a spring and enthusiasm in her manner that had not been seen since, well... you know.

Just before he left work for home, Mr. Kelley was handed a note from Tina, his after school cashier, from his wife. It read, "Please pick up some French vanilla ice cream with cherry halves for dessert tonight. Don't forget!" Mr. Kelley blanched and felt a shiver course through his spine.

Slowly stooping, he opened the small refrigerator under his work counter which was used to store medicines marked "Antibiotics - Keep Refrigerated." He removed the single half gallon of ice cream he had purchased at lunch and stored there until just now. It was Angel's favorite. Especially when covered with cherry halves, like those in the jar on the work counter.

After supper, which was for the first time in oh, so long, set for three, both Kelleys silently prepared for Angel's party. Both knew with clear certainty that she would come when the lights were extinguished and the candles adorning the cake were lit. They sang "Happy Birthday" to Angel's empty plate, and fell silent in patient anticipation. In the dim light, they heard her giggle and saw her faint form just beyond the softly glowing radiance of the candles which decorated the cake.

Both silently cried, and smiled as they had not smiled in many, many months, and beheld.

And Angel smiled back.

When Kids Play at Night

You're too grown up so we really don't expect you to believe us. You're too locked into that world of schedules and have-tos and making money. You have forgotten that a stick can be a stick...or it can be a king's scepter, or a sword, or a baton, or a spear. It can be anything you can think of. You've forgotten that the mind isn't just for thinking but it's also for playing and imagining.

Imagine seeing ghosts.

We've been seeing ghosts a lot lately. We know what they are, even if we don't know how it can be or why they are around. We see them and we know what we see. We don't expect you to believe that because, you'll say, "You're just kids. What do you know?"

Well, we don't know about kissing or sex stuff or jobs. But we know a ghost when we see one.

Summer is my favorite time of the year. Having no school is great enough. But being able to play outside with the kids who live around me on Paw Paw and to play at night is just too good. Way I see it; nights are for kids to play in.

Our favorite game is Ghosts in the Graveyard. It's best played in the time just before it gets really dark. That hour or so when the shadows cover the woods and the night bugs come out. Ghosts in the Graveyard is best when you can see a little bit. We play it in the fields along our lake. There is a strip of land that we all own, at least our parents own, that's our shared community land. It stretches around the lake in a big circle and anyone can play on it. It's the best part of living on Paw Paw Lake because no one can chase us off "the lake loop," as we call it.

To play Ghosts, one person is "it" and goes off to hide. They can hide anywhere on the loop and that's fair. They don't have to be in sight. The rest of us then wander and try to find the kid who is hiding. That kid's the ghost. Wherever we start the game is the "safe" spot and when you're in there no one can catch you and the ghost can't come into it. So, the ghost is hiding and we go out to find it before it finds us. It's a great game because in that dusky light it's easy for the ghost to jump out and scare you silly.

Now, the ghost can catch you if you get close and it touches you. But if you see it coming, you can run to the safe area and it can't tag you to be it next. As you run to the safe spot you shout, "Ghosts in the Graveyard. Ghosts in the Graveyard," to warn the other kids that it's on the prowl. If it catches you, you have to go and wait for the end of the game. It's the best game and we play it almost every night that it isn't raining or too many aren't on vacation or at camp.

Now, I'm going to be fourteen late this summer and my dad says I'm too old to keep playing with the younger kids out here, but I think he's wrong. Fourteen isn't old and my best friend, Kurt, is only twelve but we have fun still.

I was the first to see the ghost from our lake. And I am not bragging. Seeing a real ghost was never anything I ever hoped for, that's for sure.

The first time the ghost came was a month ago, right after school was out. Some of us had been playing Ghosts for a while in the final weeks of school, but not for very long because our parents made us go in early since we still had school. We called it the warm up games and would play long games on the weekends some. When school was out, we would begin the real games, making sure that everyone in the neighborhood was there with us.

Most of the gang was still in town so we had a pretty big bunch playing. It was our initiation game, when we made sure the new kids in the neighborhood got invited to join us and we get one of the families to have a cook-out with hot dogs or something for the first time. Kurt's mom, his dad doesn't live with them anymore but they aren't divorced, said we could go to his house for the initiation night and she called all the parents and made sure all the kids were invited. I bet there was twenty or more that night. It was weird because I was born here and I didn't actually know maybe seven of the new kids. We always let them play at first, because a kid can be a jerk at school and great at playing games, so it's important that we give the new kids a chance. One kids, goes by Jon Boy, had great promise as a future champion.

So, after we eat and act gross with our food, we get everyone together and make them listen serious. We hate it when the rules get changed or overlooked so we tell the rules slowly and make sure everyone understands. If they cheat or get it wrong, it can ruin the whole night with fights or kids getting mad. I hate that so we tell the rules complete for the first few games.

Anyway, after Kurt's mom fed us we all walked to the picnic area that's part of the loop and I told the rules like we do. Kurt helped me a little because I sometimes jump ahead but he's the kind that says things in order. I tell them because I'm the oldest and the little kids will listen. With him being twelve, it's just too close in age and the kids sometimes act like they don't have to listen to him. Plus, I'm about the biggest and Kurt's kind of a shrimp still.

Now, it was getting just the right dark, and Kurt said it was the almost longest day of the year, so we knew we would have a great game. As a goofy thing, I made everyone hold hands and we said a pre-game chant that I saw on a TV mystery where these witches were calling for dead spirits. I told them all to say, "Come Great Spirit of the lake and show yourself to us," and we all did. On the show, the witches were calling for some devil or something so my chant was different but kind of like theirs.

We started the game; Cheryl, the oldest girl in the neighborhood, was the ghost so we gave her a long time to hide. Cheryl is a really neat girl and she's just past thirteen. If I had a girlfriend, which I don't, I'd like it to be Cheryl. She's smart, and she is very good at school stuff, but she also takes some kinds of karate called Kuk Sul so that balances out.

Cheryl almost always hides about half way across the lake in the area where the woods come down to the lake, so Kurt and I figured we would stay together to watch how the new kids played. We went around the lake the opposite way from where Cheryl went when we started to count to 200. We do it loud so the ghost can hear us. Kurt and I knew she didn't double back because there's a sliver of space she would have to cross if she did that you can see real clear. She had on a yellow shirt and we didn't see it pass the sliver so we knew she was going to her place.

The game went along real good and the new kids were joining right in like pros, making me and Kurt feel this would a good summer of games. I told Kurt that the practice games were paying off. We walked out to the bridge that goes over the lake spillway and sat on the small wooden walk to watch the game around the lake. Kids were screaming and laughing. We could smell someone grilling burgers up the street. Jessica and Jerry, the Kotnik twins, must have let their dog loose because we could hear it barking as it chased kids through the woods. Cheryl was jogging through the far side of the lake in pursuit of someone we couldn't see. Being the bosses of the game, we like to watch over it in the early weeks. We were just getting up to go back into the game when we saw "her". But at that time, we didn't know it was a lady. It was, however, certainly a ghost.

I saw it first but couldn't quite understand what I was seeing. My mind tried to see fog or some kind of mist off of the lake, but my eyes knew it was seeing a spook come out of the lake. It was walking toward us but not really seeing us. Later Kurt said it looked to him like it was seeing something outside of our time so it seemed unusual for the ghost to be seen by us in our time – if that makes any sense. Anyway, she walked through the swimming part of the lake and out of the water by the beach just as natural as you could ever think. I noticed she made no waves in the water. I was as still as could be.

My mind was still fighting with my eyes when I realized Kurt was flying across the back yards toward my house screaming and shouting for me to run. That was when my eyes won out and my mind accepted what it was seeing. It was plainly a ghost.

I never looked back and caught up with Kurt pretty quick. At fourteen, I'm pretty fast and getting strong. He grabbed my tee shirt as I passed him and I grabbed his arm. We fell. Together we looked back and could still see her as she kept walking, now across the sandy beach into Mr. Wrisley's yard. His yard is the closest to the beach and he gets grouchy when we come too close to his tree line, which he says is at the end of the community area. I could only think that the ghost might lose the battle if she was to get tangled in a fight with old man Wris. Of course, I wasn't admitting yet we were seeing a real ghost. I needed to talk to Kurt about it first and we were too scared to do any talking at that moment. Kurt was yammering "Oh God, oh God" over and over.

Then the ghost just evaporated. It was gone like it had never been there.

We sat there in the wet field, our butts soaking up the night dew, and just stared at the spot we last saw her. That was until Cheryl ran up to us from behind and screamed, "Got you!" Why, we both nearly died right there.

I jumped to my feet and screamed at her some not nice words and Kurt busted into tears right there in front of all the kids. Cheryl got real mad and pushed me on the chest telling me that I was no better than the rest and if I got caught, I was caught. Kurt kept crying and rubbing his eyes and went home. Cheryl followed him apologizing even though she didn't know why. Everyone just kind of broke up and went home. And I followed, looking back over my shoulder about every other step.

I read once in school that people in shock sometimes sleep like on medicine because their minds are too full of stress. I slept all night until almost noon that next day, missing the Saturday cartoons. Mom got me up when Kurt came over and she let him come up to my room.

He looked real bad. His eyes were red and swollen from crying and he had dark half circles under his eyes.

He asked me if we really saw it and I said I didn't know and never want to know. He said that maybe it wasn't a hurting ghost and just some lost spirit moving to Heaven. I thought about this and decided I couldn't ask Sister Mary Serenity at our Saturday catechism. She wasn't the kind to discuss our many "what ifs," which she would think this was. I told Kurt he was probably right and we wouldn't see it again. But neither of us looked too sure.

All that day we stayed inside. When it started to get dark some of the kids came over but we told them we were watching TV movies and didn't want to play. They looked at us like we were nuts, and maybe we were. We could hear them playing in the back until it was too dark to see. We both wanted to be with them. Neither of us said a word about what we saw.

When you're young like us, it takes a pretty big thing to keep you in very long. After church that Sunday, Kurt and I went on a bike ride on our road. We saw Cheryl and I told her that I was sorry for telling her off. She said she wished she hadn't pushed on me and we told her to get her bike and we'd ride. When she went into her garage, I asked Kurt if we should tell her. He said, "Like she'd believe us," and we left it alone.

That evening Cheryl said the kids were planning a new game of Ghosts. I asked her how it went the night before and she said the new kids and the younger kids who were old enough to play now did pretty good. Then she cocked her head at an interesting angle and said it didn't seem right without me. After a second she added the words "and Kurt" but I could tell they were extra. I never looked at Cheryl quite the same after that. She looked, well…pretty. I could feel my cheeks blush, but Kurt didn't seem to notice, so that was good.

We did play that night but Kurt and I played up from the lake. We both love being the ghost, but neither of us volunteered, and we both made sure we weren't caught, because the first caught had to be the ghost in the next round. That evening the only ghost seen were the kids who were "it." I was very relieved.

The ghost came back a few nights later, and this time Cheryl saw it, too. Kurt was off with the kids around the wooded area of the lake chasing them because he was it, so I hung near Cheryl. She saw it first and sucked in a big lungful of air. Hearing her I knew what she was seeing and tried not to look to the lake but my head turned on its own without my brain saying it could. The ghost was walking up from the lake, head and upper body showing when I saw it. No ripples in the water, it just walked on out and up the beach. This time, I was farther away than when I saw it with Kurt, but it filled my eyes as though I was standing next to it. Neither of us ran, and when it disappeared, we noticed we were clinging to each other in a hug. I liked the feeling and was not the first one to pull away. To think that was the last summer I hated girls.

Cheryl asked me if we really saw it, so I told her what had happened with me and Kurt the night he started crying when I yelled at her. She didn't say anything and kept her eye on the spot where it vanished. Then we went back to the safe spot while the rest of the kids played the game. My heart wasn't into playing, and Kurt wanted to keep playing, so I walked Cheryl home and wished there had been someone to walk me home from her house in the dark. There aren't any street lights in our neighborhood, but most of the neighbors leave their front lights on for us kids, which helped me some.

Kurt and Cheryl and I sat around the next day and tried to figure this out among ourselves. We knew what we had seen, and we knew that there was no way to understand it, but we talked about it all day anyway. After lunch, we asked our moms or baby-sitters if we could ride our bikes up to the Bainbridge Library, which we are allowed to do because it's not dangerous to bike there and only about three miles away. Cheryl thought we might find some books on the subject of ghosts.

We left the library hours later with our backpacks filled with ghost stories and books claiming to be true on the subject. Some of the stories were real scary, and the "true" accounts seemed mostly stupid, like those grocery store papers at the checkout. But we read them and put torn up strips from old comic books (no super hero books, of course, but those comics of real books that grandmas like to give you for your birthday) to mark pages for the others to read. We thought we gathered quite a lot of knowledge on the subject.

Most seemed to say that ghosts were disembodied spirits, which means the person's soul after it leaves the dead body, that were trapped in this life in confusion because of a sudden death. They were here still thinking they were alive. Some said that ghosts were still on earth to work out some important task or thing left not done. These ghosts go to Heaven when they get it worked out, but no one seemed to offer how a ghost gets important stuff worked out, so I had a hard time believing this explanation.

Some told of ghosts that throw things or cause trouble. Some talked about ghosts that attach themselves to a person for some reason, and one guy claimed that they can haunt objects and be passed on from owner to owner when the chair or table was sold or given away. Kurt loved this one and said wouldn't it be the worst kind of luck to pick up a chest or table from the side of the road on trash pick up day only to find it haunted by a ghost. That would be so creepy.

We knew a lot about ghosts now, but we still had no idea about what we were seeing. Cheryl wanted to tell her mom, who is a pretty cool mom, but Kurt thought we should wait. He wondered if adults could see this kind of thing, because they were always so quick to decide that something wasn't so. I agreed with him, and Cheryl said she'd keep quiet.

After supper, we knew the plan was to play Ghosts again. Cheryl thought we could get the kids to play something less scary like flashlight tag or kick the can or soccer. Kurt and I like those games, too, so we agreed. Of course, we were assuming that the ghost we were seeing was somehow attached to our game. We were really wrong on that one.

As games will, our soccer game, which was what we were playing as light left the evening sky, kind of migrated from our backyards and down to the lake without anyone noticing. We were really lost in the game, playing a version that Kurt invented when we were kids that plays four teams against the other three with each team trying to win. It's a form of free-for-all and no team ever wins. But it's very fun. We were in the stretch of community land just up from the beach and behind Mr. Wrisley's tree line. So when the other kids saw the ghost we shouldn't have been surprised, but we were.

I guess the three of us assumed that we were the only ones that could see the ghost. Turned out little Hanna Hixon, only nine, saw it first and just stopped dead in the middle of the game as still as a tree. Cheryl nearly collided with her and went to tell her off — she's really good at that. Cheryl happened to glance where Hanna was looking. In seconds, we were all silently watching the ghost walk out of the lake toward us. Our game ball rolled slowly down the sloped bank toward it as the presence came nearer and nearer.

No one remembers what unfroze us. In a flash, we were all scattering in every direction, except toward the lake. I still marvel that no one screamed. We just went as fast as we could in whatever direction our parents were. Me, Kurt, and Cheryl darted to my house together. Cheryl beat us both by half a block.

None of us talked about it. What was there to say? Cheryl did mention that the ghost was a lady ghost and that she was naked. She had noticed boobs which was surprising to me because I thought a guy might notice that before a girl. Cheryl got all huffy and said it was only logical that she would notice them because she had them herself. Kurt and I giggled, covering our faces with our hands as Cheryl blushed. Neither of us thought it wise to say what we were thinking which was, "Oh yeah? Prove it."

I could tell of the nights that followed and the other sightings of the ghost but there isn't anything new to tell. Cheryl was right in that the ghost was a she and she was naked. Kurt and I figured out that the lady was becoming easier to see each time we saw her. She remained ghostly, whitish-gray and solid and see-through all at the same time, but she seemed to become more solid every time we saw her.

The whole neighborhood knows we have a ghost. The kids, I mean. Lately, we sit on the bridge and watch her come up from out of the lake in silence, like we do when the meteor showers come in August, and we sit on our backs watching for shooting stars. It's sort of unnatural for kids to be together in such a large group and not talk and pick on someone. But we just watch for her and, after she fades out, we go to our homes.

I figure she's a wife or lover who drowned in the lake and was never found. Cheryl and Kurt say she was murdered by Mr. Wrisley and she's getting up the force or ghost power to go and get him. The littler kids think she's an angel or some kind of lake spirit, but I think they just want her to be anything but what she is. Nope, it's clear that she is a genuine ghost.

Cheryl did tell her mom last week. We all agreed that her mom was the logical test case. I always liked Cheryl's mom because she told us to call her Suzie. She grew up on Branch Street, just like me and had a funny last name of Steines. She laughed and didn't say anything. It was almost like she already knew because her laugh wasn't making fun of us. It was uncomfortable laughing, like when you try to cover up something, like the laugh kids get when they figure out about Santa but don't want to let their parents know for sure because maybe they won't give you so many toys at Christmas. She wouldn't talk about it, but she did listen to our stories. Seemed almost like she had a story of her own.

Anyway, we still play Ghosts in the Graveyard and other night games, but not so much on that side of the lake. When it gets real dark, we move up to the backyards, closer to our folks. We aren't really that scared of the ghost lady, but if she can exist, who knows what else might be in the lake or the woods.

I don't expect any adult to believe this. I wrote this down for me, mostly. I can see that kids begin to forget as they get older. My older sister did. She's too "mature" to watch cartoons and spends her time on the phone talking about hairstyles and how nice so-and-so's behind looks in jeans. I know I'll keep growing up, but I hope I don't get too old. When you're old, you forget what it's like to be a kid. And, far as we can tell, only kids see the lady ghost. And she's worth seeing for as long as I can keep seeing her.

The Fourth Thursday in November

Responded to call at 15:35 h. 43 Paw Paw Lake Dr. Neighbors called in report having not seen resident in many days. Suspected problems with resident reported as being ill. Entered residence after no response from bell or knocking. Visual survey through windows showed concerning details in kitchen, which was in heavy disarray. We called for backup and forced our entry onto the premises.

Katie Guttmann's dead body was not discovered until the Tuesday following Thanksgiving when a co-worker reported her absence from work to the police. When the officials entered her home, they were overwhelmed by the sight of Katie sitting erect and dead at the head of a table laden with food and drink. She had obviously died alone, yet the table was set for some dozen and a half guests. The food was heaping, yet completely uneaten.

Katie Guttmann was a study in inconsistencies and contradictions. She had two eyes, but one was blue-green, the other brown. She had an upturned button nose, much like a runway model, yet her ears were almost gargantuan and needed to be carefully hidden by her layered hair. Her smile was a natural part of her full ruby lips, yet it seemed to be a strain - a frown that pulled up at the corners. Her laugh was full and loud, but it never seemed to be genuine, as if humor never entered.

Professionally, Katie had studied to be a teacher, hoping to teach college in the Education Department. She had worked for eleven years in that very place - as a secretary. She drove a Ford, although her co-worker's father owned a Toyota dealership and boasted continually of the deal he wanted to offer her. In truth, he probably would have given her a car at his cost just to get her out of an American auto.

Other discrepancies filled her life, her love of cats and yet at one time owning a dog. Her desire to be fully independent, yet living in the same room she occupied as a child in her parent's home. Her attraction to men of African-American descent, yet never dating outside of her ethnic persuasion, being Jewish. She was aware of these physic arguments within her being, yet she was at a loss as to how to make any changes.

As Halloween faded and cold weather filled the days, she became depressed and inattentive to her world. Like most of her acquaintances, she was critical of the rush of merchant-imposed holiday displays, each attempting to extract her last spending dollar for some useless, glittering babble. As a Jewish child, these matters were not of her world and, therefore, of no concern. However, her teen years till her late twenties were spent recognizing, but never celebrating, the Christian observances. Her father died of a stroke when she was nine and her mother re-married a pretty good guy two years later. Even though Shane was a non-practicing Catholic, he insisted that his family at least share the material aspects of the celebration of the birth of Christ. So, another inconsistency and contradiction crept into her life. Judaism was displaced by a nativity. With this departure went her childhood dreams of being a cantor at Temple. Singing in a Christian choir did not have the same appeal. Besides, her parents only attended church at the two high holidays of Christmas and Easter. Spiritual matters were of little concern in her mother's new family.

After her mother's remarriage, Katie and the new blended family lived in a nice enough ranch home on Paw Paw Lake. She lived there with her maternal grandfather, her mom and step-dad, and his twin sons, who were older and rarely home. After-school jobs, band practice, school sports all seemed to relegate them to being night residents.

When she was eleven, the twins left for college, leaving Katie the run of the house until she did the same. Sadly, love evaded her each time she tried it. After graduating from college she moved home for what she expected to be a brief time. Now, just over thirty years old, she owned the house free and clear.

Her step-father died in a freak accident at work her first year of college. Shane owned a high end furniture store in town. One day he decided to inventory his current stock which was held in a warehouse in nearby Solon. His childhood baseball buddy, Stevie, who was the tow motor operator, accidentally backed into a storage rack, causing it to overturn along with the six sofas it was holding. No one knew that under the pile of couches lay one very dead owner. In fact, the frustrated, unsuspecting crew decided not to resolve the mess until after they broke for lunch.

Her two step-brothers were killed in non-related accidents as she struggled to finish her senior year in college. Both died in car accidents in the excessive snows of the lake effect region east of Cleveland. Drew was killed in a head-on when a motorist lost control and swerved left of center; Mikey slipped into a tree which only dented the car but somehow snapped his neck.

Her grandfather died of old age a year after graduation. His death was peaceful and expected, occurring in his sleep. She took great comfort in the knowledge that Papa was with Abraham and the Patriarchs.

Her mother's death was by her own hand. Having lost a second husband, she could no longer face life. Both of her men had left her with more money than she could ever reasonably spend, but her demons were not in dollars, they were in the fearful clutches of loneliness. Dependent upon male companions, yet unwilling to set out to find a mate for a third time, she took a concoction of prescription drugs and drifted into death through the warm waves of ever deeper sleep that washed over her until the end. Not wanting to contaminate the house, she determined that the lawn chair in the garage, which she set up next to her new Caddie, would make a nice place to die. Lemonade in hand, she shoveled the pills in and let the pharmacy do what it does so well. Thankfully, a neighbor discovered her, very dead, in the garage as he returned some garden tools borrowed the previous summer. At least Katie was spared the horror of such a discovery.

And now, standing alone in her empty house on the lake, staring with unseeing eyes at the remainders of early snows of November, Katie struggled with the drama of her own loneliness. She did not know what to do about Thanksgiving, now only three days away. Should she ignore it and find some comfort in a nice bottle of red wine? Or should she make the elaborate meal for herself in defiance to the mind numbing life she daily faced? The skies darkened as she stood motionless in the picture window of her silent home. Wordlessly, she mouthed that the house had become her living tomb.

With a blare of unnatural sound, her phone brought her to aware-ness. Fumbling with the receiver, her heart racing from the startling, electronic beeping, she wondered who would be calling. She had no friends, no lovers, no relatives, and no reason to own a phone. After her tentative "Hello?" she quickly determined it was a wrong number, and hung up. Some call it solitude, but to Katie it was isolation.

A few hours later, after watching mindless and humor-deprived sitcoms, she went to bed.

In her dreams, she reconstructed Thanksgivings from the past. Her house was filled with family and friends, which was strange because she knew only a few of those she spoke to. The table was overflow-ing with food and fine settings of china. Wines of exquisite quality were relished from beautiful hand blown glasses of infinite delicacy. Laughter and interesting talk filled the meal and the hours following. No one seemed tired or willing to break the magic of the day, and so she dreamed on and on into the morning. And, perhaps what was the strangest element of the night, the dream remained clear and ever before her as she prepared to face another day of answering phones at the college.

This Tuesday before Thanksgiving was a wonder due to the dream. It was as if the dream had ushered her into a new life. People were friendly and engaging. Work was meaningful and suddenly important. The faculty and students were a miracle, so intelligent and wonderful. The end of the day held the most delight, when three invitations came to her to spend Thanksgiving Thursday with three families of co-workers. Laughing at the joy of being remembered, she declined each one, begging off because of the dream, which she kept to herself.

In her heart, she knew that her family would join her for the holiday, and she wanted to be home when they came.

Wednesday was less busy than usual as so many students and even a few staff and teachers departed for Thanksgiving gatherings a bit early. A threat of snow, and the promise of a break from study and work, provided sufficient excuse for many to abandon the responsibilities of higher education and head to a thousand different destinations.

The reduced work suited Katie just fine, as she had a special dinner to prepare. Under her desk blotter, she added items to a large purple Post-It which had steadily grown throughout the day. After work, she spent over an hour filling her shopping cart with the standards of the Thanksgiving, as well as a few ethnic Jewish favorites to make Thanksgiving a truly meaningful meal.

She cleaned and stuffed the turkey and set it in the refrigerator for morning. Sweet potatoes and marshmallows, a large salad, various vegetables, and a number of special treats, like red candied apple circles and brown bread pudding were made in advance and cooled for the evening in the fridge. She baked fresh rolls, liberally tasting her efforts. With a curious smile, she made matzo balls for the first course soup. In the background, her stereo played Baroque classics to fill the space of the rooms before her guests arrived.

Never once did she consider the absurdity of her expectations. In life, she never really cared for her family much, nor did she feel cared for by them. But something in the dream powered her expectations. She never thought that she was anticipating the dead of her family to come and eat her labor of love on this most American of all observances, yet the dream seemed so real, making her believe that they would come.

She made a mental note that she would need to insert the three table leaves so that all could be together. She'd do that in the morning as the turkey browned. Right now, it was time for a bottle of white zinfandel and a dozen or so scented candles around the edge of a nearly scalding hot bath. She had a ton of work still to attend to, but morning would be soon enough. It was time to relax in the sense of family she was so glad to welcome into her soul - for the first time ever.

Her dreams were again filled with her family and her new friends as each one hugged her and shared a lengthy bit of conversation. Her kitchen was again turned over to her mother, its true queen, as the dream family cooked the meal together. Over the course of the night, she learned that the new friends, who accepted her with no pretense, were some of the neighbors who had occupied the area over the years past. Not once did it occur to Katie that all of her dream companions were dead.

Morning brought her to full wakefulness with the rise of the sun. She popped the turkey into the oven with completion aimed at 2pm. With obvious difficulty, she stretched the large oak table to its full capacity and set the three matching inserts into place. Chairs were mismatched and from every part of the house, but there was sufficient room for everyone. Liberally sipping from a wine glass laden with pleasure, she set the table, first spreading the family heirloom tablecloth which had been passed down to her by default. Papa had remarked that it was Nana's most adored possession. Katie remembered that Nana had been in the dreams. She had never met Nana, since she had died before Katie entered the world. Her best china and silver were laid with care and love. She hoped that her love would equal the love that would soon be shared over the meal.

Tasks clicked off in rapid succession, with no complications or hitches. By 12:30, all was ready, except for the browning bird. Slipping off her shoes, Katie decided to nap for a half hour before finishing.

Katie was awakened from her nap as the door bell rang with the arrival of her first guests. Gratefully, she thanked her mother for greeting the first few and allowing her to sleep a bit longer. Her real father and her step-dad were entertaining the arrivals, serving wine and some very nice hors d'oeuvres that one among the company had considerately brought. The air was filled with sound and aroma; laughter and cooking mingled to enrich the senses. Katie beamed as she felt the waves of family companionship wash over her.

The meal was served at two o'clock on the dot. Both of her fathers gave thanks with respect for their own faith traditions, with proper homage to the other. The table was filled with food, the chairs with family and guests. For the first time in her life, Katie Guttmann felt at home. A tear of joy and contentment slipped down her cheek, noticed only by her mother, who reached out and took the single drop onto her own napkin.

And so the day flowed into night and the night into eternity.

Sgt MG Swarts, the lead of the emergency attendants investigating the tipoff phone call from a neighbor some days later, commented that it looked as though she prepared for the whole neighborhood, yet was certainly alone. It made no sense to him that someone should cook for so many and for no one to be there. Obviously, there were no guests coming, or they would have discovered, or been present at, the death.

The other attendants nodded in agreement but remained silent.

Everyone's thoughts were filled with the inconsistencies and contradictions of the event. It made no sense to anyone, but, in truth, so little did anymore.

After the final photos were taken to support the report of T. Guttmann's natural passing, the emergency responders left with the body and closed the door. Behind them the sound of merriment and family celebration seemed to fill the room in a whisper. Had any of the team looked again, perhaps they would have seen the celebration of gratitude that was an eternal glow of the meal eaten forever, on the fourth Thursday in November.

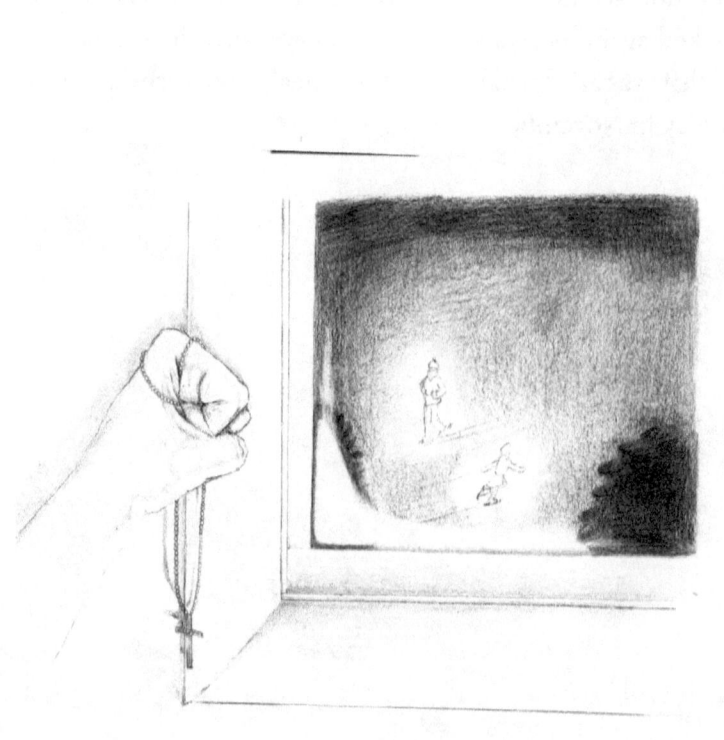

Night Skaters

Murder came all too easy for Frank. It had become his occasional hobby. Certainly, he would murder more. But missing people eventually led back to some related and shared factor. He had been lucky to this point. Eight glorious murders over something better than twenty five years. And never a knock on his door to question him.

Frank lived on the last house on Lake Drive, the single road which ran through Paw Paw Lake with a turning circle in front of his house. His little Cape Cod home faced the lake in a remote view which shielded him from the other houses on the lake. His closest neighbor was out and around the bend behind him. It was the perfect setting for a recluse like he pretended to be.

The previous owners were one of the original "settlers" in Paw Paw, building the house in the 30's and living there for only a few decades. The standard residential habit was to stay almost forever. But the Smiths or Jones or whatever the heck their name was, decided to retire to Florida and only stayed through the mid 50's. Frank was a young, single, military man back from Korea and as the 50's built momentum; he decided he needed a house because that's what everybody said. "Don't pay rent when you can invest in your own property!" his banker uncle told him.

So Frank bought the house directly from the whomevers. He even worked out a sweet deal where he paid them directly. No bank, no loan, no interest. Nothing but a personal check for $83.67 a month for twenty years. And, to make matters even sweeter, the idiots even deeded the house to him up front so he could benefit from the ownership. In their will, they left the house to him if they died and they told him so. They had no kids and kind of thought it appropriate to be help a young Marine returned home. Their largesse cost them their lives.

Frank went to work with the State of Ohio roads service as an inspector. He made great money and was assured of a wonderful future. The measly amount that he paid to the Joneses, (or was it Smiths?) was meaningless. But it was just too enticing to think how easily he could own the house free and clear.

In his second year, he took his vacation time and drove to Florida to visit the Smiths unannounced (I think it was Jones - why can't I remember?). He told none of his co-workers where he was off to. No one knew and he would tell his very few friends that he stayed home and slept for two weeks. Who could prove different?

It was too easy to kill them in their home. In Korea there was the hunt and being hunted. The risk that death could come from any hollow point. This was just an early graduation party for a couple of old codgers. Making it look like a suicide was an idea that came to him on the drive down. It was so perfect he even him impressed himself.

He put them to sleep with sleeping gas he lifted from a small dentist's office he broke into in northern Florida in some off-the-main-drag, fly-speck town. He gassed them in their home and placed them in their car in the garage, leaving it running with them in it. They never rallied. They just slept their way into eternity. As he left them in their Buick coffin, he thanked them for the house and checked himself into a local hotel to follow the discovery and investigation.

Sure enough, they were discovered by the milk man when two days' milk went untouched. The papers listed it as a suicide of two aging lovers who must have been facing fears of the end. Frank figured that entwining their fingers together before shutting them into the running car prompted the lovers' reference. After a week, he headed north to his soon to be paid-off house.

It takes time to process the estate of folks with no family, so Frank continued to send his monthly payment. After three months, he received notice that the Smiths/Jones/Whatevers had died unexpectedly, leaving their house to him. The courts estimated that final papers would be completed shortly. His checks were returned.

Frank made much noise to the court secretary and the receptionist of the JonesSmiths' attorney's office when they called for their various reasons attached to the deaths. He expressed his complete shock and choked back some serious fake tears. It was a great act, fully convincing. Both women, bless their hearts, sent him letters of condolence at this unexpected and devastating loss. They assured him, in their separate ways, that God would help him through this most difficult time.

Six months to the day of his visit to the Sunshine State, the final papers were in his possession, confirming the cancellation of his debt as listed in the settlement of estate. A bonus was also enclosed. As there was no next of kin to be found, half of the estate was to be given to him, in cash, following the sheriff's sale of the Florida property. Frank chuckled at his convincing act to the two women who made this all possible, persistently suggesting to their bosses that this was the right thing to do. Frank sent them both two dozen long stemmed red roses and a check for $100 with his heartfelt thanks. It was, in his opinion, the unexpected bonuses of life that gave it dimension and character.

It was some time before Frank indulged in his second murderous outing. Almost eight years passed before he killed his boss at the county office of the state department. Mr. Hank Holms was intolerable as roads department supervisor. He was a huge man of considerable bulk, with foul breath and even fouler management abilities. Frank hated him with a dearness that caused him to attend to Holms as a lover might watch her beloved.

No inspiration came to Frank as to how he might dispose of Holms in a manner befitting his magnitude in body and position. So, he simple ran him over on one of the road construction jobs in front of everyone.

Frank had been assigned to drive his boss to a job site, a major culvert project under what would soon become a primary roadway cutting through the county east to west. His plotting had been thwarted at every angle. To just kill him would be to bring Frank immediately under suspicion. So, over time, Frank took the "suck up" posture and openly supported and idealized Holms at every opportunity. Holms noticed Frank's endorsements and began to respond by making Frank his favored supervisor. They spent a great deal of time together on the jobs. It was easy for Frank to run him over. It just was a matter of waiting for the right time and place.

When it came, it was the most natural execution imaginable. While waiting in the truck for Mr. Holms to finish his instructions to the job foreman, Frank shifted the truck from reverse to drive. In the middle of the conversation, Frank yelled to the two men that he was going to turn the truck around and reminded Holms that lunch today was on him in celebration of his supervisor's belated birthday.

As Hank was telling his foreman what a great guy Frank was, Frank turned in his seat to look out of the rear window and hit the gas. Hard. The truck slammed into Hank and the other guy, knocking them off of the road foundation into the culvert spillway. Mr. Hank Holms died from the twelve-foot drop onto large, broken slabs of concrete which served as erosion protection. Frank held him in his arms, crying like a child, as the dying Hank told him they'd have to wait for his birthday lunch. The other man survived with a broken leg and arm. Plenty of witnesses saw the terrible freak accident; a stupid mistake that Frank would have to live with all his days.

The papers spoke more about Frank's horrible ordeal, accidentally killing his boss and friend, than they did about Hank's contribution to the county roadways. Frank received more sympathy cards than Hank's widow. He chuckled at each one. That blimp was gone, and he'd likely get a promotion.

It turned out that he didn't get the advancement, but that was OK. He'd played a dangerous game twice in eight years, claiming three victims. Each death made his life more comfortable and enjoyable. The feeling of pulling off murder was an exhilarating boost to one's attitude of superiority.

In the early 70's Frank struck again, killing a "hippie chick," as she called herself, who was camping behind his house in the woods. She was alone, experiencing nature, naked as God intended, and deeply wanting to "make it" with Frank, as she put it.

Frank was not hugely interested in sex. He rarely had sexual feelings. But how does one resist a naked hippie who so graciously offers herself. While others might have shared a post coitus cigarette under the fading light of the summer sky, Frank, instead, turned her on her stomach and strangled her from behind. After dark, he wedged her body deep in the spillway of Paw Paw Lake, where she would swim undiscovered through the whole Disco era. By the time she was discovered, Frank had polished off his fifth victim.

Number five was a hitchhiker named John who was "seeing the country on the front seats of other people's cars." Frank hadn't intended to kill him when he picked him up, but the idea edged itself into his mind. It was a "no reason" murder, but he enjoyed it just the same. John was laid to rest on a southern Ohio picnic table at a road side rest stop. The Cleveland papers didn't even carry the story.

Six and seven were killed the day that Frank discovered he had lung cancer and was told that half of his left lung would become a medical school specimen. Facing this dangerous and horrible operation left Frank quite "edgy." He hiked up the river which linked the three lakes of this end of Geauga County and murdered a couple in their home. The papers reported this brutal slaying in detail for weeks. No suspects. No motive. No clues. Later Frank figured he was lucky that it had been raining that late autumn night. His trek up the slippery river bank and into their ranch home was wiped out by the hard rain. Before killing them, he watched them through their picture window, which offered a stunning view of the woods and river valley below. Removing his shoes and socks, he entered through the garage, where he dried his wet feet thoroughly on the Mr.'s golf towels. After killing them he took his shoes and socks, as well as the golf towels, and walked home.

This one worried him, as he could not recall details. But the papers eventually noted that no clues were forthcoming from the crime scene. By winter's end, he relaxed and unloaded his shotgun, which he kept handy if problems resulting from his spontaneous adventure ever presented themselves at his front door.

His cancer operation was a success, and the subsequent chemo was not as rough as expected. Removing the diseased section of lung made him feel renewed.

Just one week before his eighth and final murder, he watched in fascination as the space shuttle exploded on national TV, replayed over and over again. It bothered him in ways he could not quite articulate. He felt jittery, unsettled.

The young woman who made the mistake of knocking on his door was a lovely public opinion worker who had been canvassing the neighborhood in search of clean air and water donations for a public lobbying group from Columbus. And, as Mr. Collins "lived on a lake he was certainly more concerned than the average citizen on the current legislation aimed at relaxing pollution standards for development builders which would cause dangerous run-off into such beautiful wonders as Paw Paw Lake." Nodding in harmony with each assertion, Frank decided that he would show her his average citizen's concern with her windpipe. He did, quickly reaching out and grabbing her throat, yanking her into his foyer, and that was that. Her grave was deep within the ancient root cellar which extended into the hill behind his house. Again, no one came looking for her. Frank was getting good at this.

Winter came to Paw Paw Lake with a vengeance just after Thanksgiving. In the plummeting temperatures, the lake froze solid and all during winter vacation Frank watched the neighborhood kids skate on the lake. They liked to scrape the snow out around the beach area, making a sizable rink. Bright hats and scarves became the targets of scampering dogs that joined the frolic of their youthful masters. Often parents would join in. Frank, now retired from the state and living on his accumulated wealth and pension, very much enjoyed the scene. He was not a neighborhood figure of prominence, preferring to stay to himself. But he could still smile at the joy so obvious in his neighbors.

The night skaters began their vigil just as the New Year broke. At first, Frank assumed they were either kids down from the other neighborhoods up the street who blatantly violated the night skate rule of Paw Paw. Too dangerous and, thus, forbidden. He was surprised to see that they did their skating in front of his house, not at the regular places.

His motto became, "who cares - let 'em drown." He mostly ignored them, hoping they'd get what they deserved. It was strange that the other neighbors from up the street said nothing even though the skaters continued night after night. Notations were made on a paper taped to his fridge of the nights they skated.

After almost two weeks of blatantly ignoring of community standards, Frank decided to give the night skaters a talking to. Bundling up on an especially cold night, he made his way to the frozen shore of the lake. The skaters ignored his shouts turned yelling turned ranting. They skated in circular silence, faces covered by winter wrappings. Frustrated, he returned to the warmth of his house. Something began to bother him.

As the days passed, Frank became aware of a few disturbing facts. First, the skaters never came when other skaters were on the lake across from him at the beach. They always came after everyone had gone to their own fires and cocoa or simply returned home. Second, he never observed them actually coming to the ice. They just appeared at the moment he looked away. Finally, never was there any sound - not on the ice, or in the neighborhood, or in the woods. Silence so loud that it hurt. And in that obscene stillness, voices within him began to question him intimately.

Now, being a man set in his ways, Frank never thought much of his accumulated murders. He killed them all in want or need and that was that. It did no good to investigate motive or reason with a hurting conscience. It was a done deal and life went on. But now, these voices were sounding familiar as they rang in his head. They spoke of the horrors he had committed on innocent lives, now snuffed out by his actions. They asked why. They demanded audience. They persisted. And they only came while the skaters were engaged in their nightly performance.

During the days, Frank would make calls to the Lake Community Association President, or the closest neighbors, or the strange fellow, Ronald, who daily walked his dog down to Frank's end of the road at 4:15 each and every night. Flaky college professor and his mutt. Frank even considered calling that Reverend Sinclair who lived up the road almost directly across the lake from him. He might have some pull.

All of his inquiries were met by concern, initially. Rules were rules and all needed to abide. The Association placed a reminder in every mailbox, but the skaters returned. Neighbors began to watch, never seeing anything. Only the professor responded in a hostile manner, pontificating some crap about how it was people like Frank who perpetrated the continuation of intimidation to our personal freedoms, collective and individual. Frank wondered what guys like this would say if big words hadn't been invented? He wondered what the professor would say looking up at Frank through the ice of ol' Paw Paw.

And each night the skaters were back. And Frank became terrified of what he now suspected. He finally stopped to count them.

There were eight skaters.

A thaw came to the area. First slowly, then, within two days, the ice had melted down to a slush which topped a thin layer of ice. Frank chucked a few fist sized rocks onto the lake and was satisfied when they fell right through the ice. For the first time in almost a month, he felt some relief. It was party time, and he decided to go out to eat and, rarity of rarities, catch a movie in town at the old movie house on East Washington St.

Upon returning home, his headlights catching the surface of the ice as he turned toward his lone house on the end of the street, he was greeted by the eight silent skaters, skating gracefully in arcs and figure eights upon the slush. Not looking at the skaters, he slowly drove into his garage, sitting for long, countless minutes in the darkness of the freezing cavern.

They were ghosts. He admitted what he knew soon after the voices came. They were the ghosts of his victims.

This stark realization in his mind quickly made him a victim of his emotions. Frank's undiagnosed socio-pathology fell to his terror. Loading his shotgun, Frank walked to the edge of the lake and began drilling the ghosts with 12-gauge bird shot. The ghosts continued their fearful recreation. The neighbors called the police. The police took Frank's gun and put him to bed. Their report indicated that nothing was seen, yet Mr. Collins persisted in his insistence that vagrants were skating on his lake.

Frank tried religion, daily praying the Rosary using his dear mother's collection of beaded strings and medallions from around the world. He stuffed them in his pockets, hung them on lamps and his rear view mirror, on his doors.

Anonymously he called a priest to inquire how much an exorcism might cost him if it was needed. The priest suggested he get a life and quit the hooch. Frank shared a collection of words not generally spoken to priests. The man of God hung up on him, only amplifying his isolation in this ordeal of his own doing.

As with any distressing calamity, this one had to end. Frank knew that the burden of action rested upon him.

His personal cleansing appeared on the pages of tablets and note-books into which he laid his full confession. It was the writing of a mad man. Yet, in spite of his incoherence, his words were totally damning.

I know they will return again, tonight. Why doesn't anyone else see them? Why are they here? They are dead. I know they are dead. I know... The police don't see them. None of the neighbors do, either. I know they will be back. But how can it be? It is impossible. God has lost control. This should not be.

His mental meandering went on for pages with much the same discourse. He was a terrified old man; aging more in the past two months. He had no way to counter the forces which had stricken him so. Unless he confessed.

He knew that no court would ever use it to put him away. You can't jail a dead man.

Frank Collins came to his own end after the ghosts appeared again, as they did every night, during the final freeze of winter. Ice returned to greet the skates of the nightly apparitions, making the scene some-how more natural. Literally bound in the Rosaries, Cross medallions, and larger crucifixes now tied to his body, Frank entered his final bat-tle equipped with the weapons of righteousness against these obvious denizens of evil. Praying fragments of high and holy liturgies he re-membered from his childhood or created in his madness, he made his way into the midst of the specters.

As he trudged toward them, his steps fell through the ice, first to his ankles and then up to knees as the shore sloped downward under the bitter, wintry waters. His personal demons drove him to go fur-ther, to get into their center. He would win as he always did.

For the first time the skaters removed their scarves and hats. They discarded their winter coats and appeared in the outfits they wore when Frank killed them. The Florida couple in shorts. The hippie chick naked and displaying her youthful and beautiful body. The family up the way in their casual lounging clothes. Hank with his hard hat and jeans. The pollster with her identification button and clipboard. The hitchhiker complete with backpack.

They faced him, eyes reborn with accusation. Lips preaching their personal gospel of retribution. Hands groping to snatch him into realization of what he had done, what he had robbed.

Miraculously, Frank crawled up on the ice in a firmer section, and slowly turned to each victim. They were pathetic, having fallen to his whims and calculations. Their existence was not only an impossibility, it was a joke. They deserved no recourse. They were his, each one. And he told them so.

Across the lake, Mrs. Gipson called the police and told what she was witnessing in the late evening sheen of the lengthening days. Emergency aid was dispatched, certain to arrive within minutes.

As patrolman C. Andrew Ramsey rounded upon the impossible sight of a crazy man wrapped in necklaces and crosses, shouting to persons not there, screaming that he would outlast them and they were as wretched in death as they had been in life, he knew his job was going to be tough. He feared walking onto the ice and wondered how this nut was staying up. He called quickly for back up.

His fears were confirmed as he watched the ice break under Collins. Weighted by the regalia of his insincere faith, he fell through and slid out of sight.

Launching into duty, Ramsey tried to crawl onto the ice, but he broke through at every attempt to get closer to the disappeared man. Soaked in freezing waters, Ramsey watched as the surface of the lake stilled, the ice solidifying before his eyes. In the silence of this watery sepulcher, he heard the backup units as they flew down Bell Street to the entrance of the community. Crossing himself, Ramsey exited the lake.

It would be weeks before the outcome of the life of Frank Collins had any meaning. To come would be an official statement by the local police and county sheriff's offices, using a Cleveland psychologist, describing how Mr. Collins entered a suicidal situation due to the immense guilt he felt from the eight murders he committed over near-ly three decades. The public would be told that he left a full confession of his deeds in his diaries. His estate would become property of the county and state for disposal. His body would be eventually interred in a small community cemetery with a plaque noting his name and years. No mourners would attend the service. Only a priest, Father Daiv, the one Collins had called for an exorcism, and the attendants of the funeral home would attend.

One strange, unrecorded, and unseen event followed on the heels of Frank Collins' drowning. Late in the night, after all the public ser-vants had left the scene and arrangements were made at the police station for equipment to reclaim the body at first light, a small group of deer ventured from the woods behind Frank's house having been frightened by a large, stray dog. In agitation, they scurried into the clearing in front of the house and froze solid for a long moment before bolting in panic.

On the frozen lake, eight forms skated unexpectedly on the lake, circling a lone man in their midst who cowered as each one skated near. Strange light glinted off of the metal badges and tabs he wore on chains about him. A fear of realization seemed to play upon his countenance as he realized he would face eternity among his persecu-tors as they weaved confusing and threatening patterns, gliding with righteous confidence at the one who took their lives.

When Lightning Strikes

The thunder did not exactly awaken Paul Fishell from his sleep - it propelled him forth. As the deafening peal faded, he launched to his feet, his heart drumming an intricate percussion solo, and moved to his bedroom door, avoiding dressing tables and discarded clothing, to intercept his terrified twins. Another blinding flash, followed immediately by the jet engine roar of the splitting air refilling the suddenly hewn vacuum, met him as he reached the door. He saw his hand clearly in that second as it began turning the knob. Total darkness returned completely hiding the door in its opening arch.

Two steps into the hall, Paul was again bathed in brilliant light as it instantly illuminated every nook and corner of the upper hall area into which spilled three bedrooms and a bath which made up the large upstairs of the Victorian home located on Paw Paw Lake. The dazzling glare of white brightness penetrated his eyes with intrusive force.

In this flash, all concern for his daughters, which would have been addressed in five short steps, was erased. Paul Fishell stopped short, his mind filled with a penetrating confusion of incomprehension. Before him he clearly saw four persons, each bearing a face covered in fear, running toward him. In the next instant, he faced only darkness.

As the rumble of the thunder rolled over his home, Paul flattened against the wall behind him as the image of the four burned into his mind. He braced for the impact of the first person, a man about his own age. As he awaited the unavoidable collision, he strained his ears to gauge the approach, hear only the fading thunder. Paralyzed with a developing fear, he did not move. Behind him, he heard his wife stir.

Another flash filled the hallway, just as he heard Maren's feet shuffle on the hardwood floor. Again, the unknown intruders were there before him, just as they had been moments before. Set in desperate flight the small group appeared to be bearing down upon him. Darkness again forced its way on the hall as thunder took over, roaring through the house. He could hear Maren nearing the doorway and one his daughters, perhaps Lindsey, cried in fear from behind her door. Tiny feet hit the floor in a run to the comforting embrace of parents.

Just as the girls' door opened, Maren entered the hall behind Paul. This Paul heard, not being able to penetrate the darkness with his vision. As the family gathered in their doorways, lightning flared again. Now all of the family was witnessing what Paul was beginning to think was the remaining particle of an interrupted dream. Before them, clearly revealed in the light, were four people caught in the stride of a fleeing dash and heading for Paul and Maren's room. From the girls' doorway, the four were seen from their sides. Incredibly, they did not seem to notice the Fishell household. Escape was obviously their only thought.

As if glued to the floor, all four Fishells stood in shock as the frenzy of the storm seemed to center upon their home. Outside the storm raged with the passion of long separated lovers, newly reunited. Inside of each of them, a very different storm seethed. A storm of immeasurable fear. Before the Mr. and Mrs. Paul Fishell family, the reenactment of another family in flight confronted them with each new lightning bolt.

Little Ellen broke the suspension of the family with a scream. Gripping her twin's wrist, she joined the four in flight with a dash of her own; blindly running into her parents. The family retreated into the parents' room. Paul slammed the door and, as children caught in the juvenile fear of a scary camp story, the Fishell family huddled behind their door under the covers of Paul and Maren's king sized bed. In fear, they cowered together, all four crying and praying for relief. As the storm drifted away, they each fell in a troubled sleep, awakening to the sound of birds and dogs barking.

Daylight eased the tensions of the family somewhat, but the Fishell women waited for Paul to peek through the door, making sure the hall was clear, before they breathed, spoke or headed for the bathroom. Rather than rising, Paul rejoined his family in bed, the door still open. Together they each gazed into the now empty hall and revisited their still vivid memories of the previous night.

Maren spoke first. "Did we all see the same thing?" she wondered.

Ellen, always the more verbose of the twins, said with caution, "Just what did you see, mom?" All eyes awaited Maren's answer.

Clearing her throat, Maren said, "I saw a family of four...well, ghosts."

Again, the four looked to the hallway in silence.

Paul, still not speaking, returned to the doorway and stood examining the small hallway. He flicked on the light, although the room needed no light being flooded by the morning sunlight, and studied each surface - walls, ceiling, floor, built-in bookcase, for some evidence of the family's shared vision. No clues gave way to his investigations.

Taking a cautious step, as one hoping to avoid a land mine, he entered the hall, keeping a hand on the door jamb as though it were a life line. He saw nothing out of the ordinary. Yet, he still would not quit searching for some bit of evidence or explanation.

Maren and the girls took up posts behind him. After a few moments, they descended the stairs to the security of the kitchen where each family member silently assisted in preparing a simple breakfast. Each knew that the topic of breakfast talk would certainly be what each one saw last night in the flashes of the storm. Breakfast set up was merely an allowance of a few moments to gather thoughts and seek to understand what was seen. Of some comfort was the knowledge that each of them had seen the same spectacle.

Over his coffee and scones, Paul told how the ghosts were there from the first burst of lightning as he went to check on Lindsey and Ellen. He told the girls that he knew the storm would awaken them and he wanted to be there to make it better. At the jaded age of nine, the girls knew that among their shared twin experiences, fearing storms was one of their top fears. A standing family joke was which parent had attended to the girls last, and whose turn it was this time should a storm break out. Maren had a way of convincing Paul that she had made the previous trip every time.

Maren jumped in when Paul noted that the four seemed to be running. She, too, thought they would run into her as they were obviously traveling in the direction of her room. Ellen added that the last person seemed to be a child being considerably shorter than the rest. Lindsey, who was obviously still the most terrified, only added that the first and second persons, both males, seemed to her to be a father and son. Maybe the third person was the mom.

As the breakfast was completed, the family agreed that the four running ghosts were a family, a mother and father with a teenage boy and a young daughter. Clothing had not been noticed and no colors were remembered by any of them. The three characteristics that the Fishell family agreed upon were that the ghosts seemed to be a family, they were in desperate flight, and they were deeply consumed by fear.

After breakfast Maren, who was not an overly religious woman, asked the family to bow as she said a prayer to God asking for protection on the family. In the quietness that followed this uncharacteristically strange act, each found their thoughts hoping that the bizarre event never be repeated.

In northeastern Ohio, spring, summer, and fall storms are as common as the unbroken weeks of snow and no sunshine in the winter. Storms may happen repeatedly and almost daily, or they may develop in a few hours and quickly dissipate. Ferocious thunderstorms are so prevalent that most Ohioans give little mind to them, except that plans will certainly be interrupted frequently throughout the warmer months. A standing joke in this region is that if the weather is not acceptable, wait a few minutes and it will surely change.

Unfortunate to the Fishell family, their first visitation of the ghostly family would be replayed only a few nights later. With numerous night-time thunderstorms, the circumstances which brought forth the first display of phantoms could be easily and often replicated. And they were.

Just as the memory of the storm which introduced the family to the specters was fading, their night was interrupted by a clap of thunder which shook the foundation of their home. Before remembering the unwelcome visitors of three nights before, Paul sat up in bed after the noise awakened him and cleared his eyes and head of sleep. Before the next burst, he glanced down to the lake upon which their house was situated, and clearly saw the sheets of rain through his yard light as they seemed to drop like a layer of water from sky to ground. He aimlessly noted that the lake would be up above its banks by morning.

Wondering if he moored his canoe well enough to resist the flood surely to occur, Paul headed to his daughters' room to check on them. As he entered the hall, half way between his room and theirs, the next revealing light of some battling gods filled the hall area and revealed again the family on the run. This time Paul was nose to nose with the lead man, the assumed father of the ghost family. With a yell, he lunged to the floor in front of his daughters' room, crawling to lean upon their door and facing the specters. His first emotion was to cry. His second though was self-chastisement in forgetting their appearance just three nights before.

Maren also screamed as she caught up with Paul in the hall in the light of the second flash of lightning. Paul hoped the girls would sleep on, in spite of his certainty they would not. *What is happening?* he wondered over and over again.

The girls joined their parents and the family watched the frozen-in-time scene for some time. Soon the Fishell family retreated between lightning flashes to the parents' room to again find some comfort and security in the clutches and tears of each other. The magnitude of the horrors revealed by the lightning was only beginning to sink in.

Morning brought a fearful numbness and a strange depression to each of the Fishell. With non-verbal pleas, each communicated that the storm generated visions were taking a toll on their sanity. Lindsey, who had always been the most sensitive of the family, looked especially drawn and troubled. Her face seemed to be dominated by dark circles which ringed her eyes. She would not talk, even when her parents tried to discuss some other topic.

A late afternoon thunderstorm came into the area. Paul hurriedly returned home from his real estate business in Chagrin, to gather his family into their Ford Explorer and take them out for an early supper. All knew that the meal was a ruse to protect the family from whatever the lightning could reveal in the upper hall. Even when the power was knocked out in the restaurant for nearly thirty minutes, the family felt safer and more secure sitting in the booth than they would have at home.

With the restored power, Maren felt her confidence being re-stored, even as the storm slowly left the area outside. As a mother seeking to protect her brood, Maren found some inner-strength which led her to gather her family together against the apparition; she simply would not allow the vision of the fleeing family of ghosts dissolve her own family.

Speaking lowly and in a monotone, she told her family that they could not continue to run from the mystery in their hall. She con-fessed that nothing in her life had ever frightened her as badly as this, but to ignore it or assume that it would not return with the next storm was ridiculous.

"I've been thinking about this, and I think that I see a pattern." she began. "These ghosts, or whatever you call them, are running from something. It's like they are trying to get away from something that is after them. Did any of you notice that the image is frozen as we see it, but that the image from a few days ago and the one we saw last night was a bit different?"

She looked at her family. Only Paul seemed to understand. He, too, had noticed that the four were in a somewhat different position than they had been. The mother had turned to look at her daughter. The son had reached to hold his father's hand.

"It seems to me that we are seeing the family as they run away from whatever it is that is making them look so terrified. They are trying to get away, but they also seem to be trying to stay together."

"Maybe a bad man is after them, mommy." Ellen offered. Lindsey only cowered more, if that could be humanly possible.

"Whatever it is, it has them afraid." Maren responded. Paul nodded.

"I think that they mean us no harm," she continued, "and I don't think that they see us. It's like we are looking in on them, or watching them on TV. They scare me, but I don't think they can hurt us."

"It seems that the lightning is somehow making them visible." Paul added, "Like holding a photo negative up to a lamp. You can see the image of the picture only if it has some light passing through it."

"But why are they in our house?" Lindsey whispered as her face was flooded with tears. Maren, sitting next to her in the booth, pulled her daughter onto her lap and let her tears flow onto her tee shirt.

"I don't know, honey. I just don't know." she answered.

After the girls were put to bed, much later that evening, Paul and Maren talked long about the phenomena on their back porch as they watched the sky for more stormy weather. Simple summer weather, usually accepted as normal, now brought fear into their hearts. Paul initiated a return to the restaurant discussion.

"Maren, I been thinking. What if something happened to these people in our home and it's being replayed for us to see. Maybe Ellen's right. Maybe some family who lived here before us had something terrible happen to them. Maybe this is part of the character of the house." He stopped to weigh her reaction but she remained silent.

"I'm a dope," he said with embarrassment.

Maren's stare was without facial evidence. Paul could not read her other than to note that the gears were turning. She looked away and scanned the darkening sky.

"Paul," she began, "you know I'm no big believer in the mystical unknown." He started to interrupt but she waved him away with a finger to his lips. "Don't be rude. Just listen to me.

"When I prayed the other morning I know you must have wondered what was going on. I'm influenced by what I see and understand and tend to dismiss what I don't grasp. But, I can't overlook what I am seeing, and it is opening me to lots of 'other world' possibilities. If I had only seen it, I could dismiss it as a dream or some bad food. But you and the twins saw it, too. In college, we looked at the impossibility of group hallucinations. This is not some shared delusion." She put her hand up to his opening mouth.

"I don't know where to put all this ghost stuff. I only know that I believe it will happen again, with the next storm. So, I see our options as being rather limited. It seems to me that we have to play this out and see where it takes us."

Paul could not look at her as he responded. "Somehow, I agree. I feel, and I know how you hate 'touchy-feely' talk, but I feel that this is a movie of sorts that we, as a family, have to witness. I bet you a dollar and a diamond that these ghosts have unfinished business with this house. Maybe they want us to know who or what killed them – 'cause I think they died together. Maybe they want us to bring them justice. Or maybe it's a warning that whoever it was that did something to them is going to get us. I don't know, Maren, but I feel we are not done with them."

In silence, they studied the skies until the mosquitoes drove them to bed.

Nearly a week passed until a strong storm woke Maren in the night. Rousing Paul, they both went to their door and watched the hall in anticipation of lightning. When it came, and as it repeated, Maren and Paul Fishell looked at the scene as it was revealed to them once again. They had to know if their theory of "one frame at a time" was valid. This time only the younger child was looking forward now. The three taller persons, the mom and dad and oldest son, were facing to the rear. Mom was looking at the daughter and the two males were looking down the stairs.

Maren whispered, "See, Paul. They are changed again. In different positions."

"And maybe the girls were right. Maybe there is something pursuing them from the steps." Paul said.

Paul got the girls, who were terrified but willing to watch and hear what their parents believed about the four phantoms. As the storm climaxed and then waned, the family watched and talked about the strange movie caught in a single frame and lit up by flares of lightning. With the last flash, the four figures seemed to fade away. Softly, Paul prayed on behalf of the family. But this prayer focused on the family they had again seen, not the one he was holding in his arms.

The following day the girls were sent to Maren's mother's house for a few days. It had been scheduled weeks earlier and both parents felt the break would do them good. Maren's mother knew the girls were afraid of storms, so Maren offered no remarks to breech the subject of lightning. She knew that a storm would likely be the girls undoing. She determined to cross that bridge if it came up.

At lunch, Paul met her at the Geauga County library to begin their research of their home. They cross-referenced the sale of the house to establish who the previous owners were. With this list of names in hand, they began researching the facts of the house. Paul, expecting it to take most of the day, called his office and told them he would not be in until the next day.

The house was part of the farm from which the Paw Paw Lake development was carved. Apparently, the vast farm holdings were the property of two brothers, both of whom had their homes built on the land. While the other house was razed by the county in the late Forties, their house, built in 1923, was original. The brother who lived there, a Harry Schlauch, never married and willed his house to his brother, Arden. Harry died in a farming accident in the mid-Thirties. Arden sold the house to a Kardos family, which began a string of thirteen owners or renters, the Fishell family being the thirteenth.

It was in 1964 that the Kotnik family purchased the home. Mr. Kotnik was an electrical contractor and Mrs. Kotnik a nurse. With their oldest son, Tyler, and their beloved but unexpected Thea, they moved in during the British Invasion of Rock and Roll. Far from their minds were these social influences. They were all enamored with the house and its darling character. The same character that drew the Fishell family to buy it.

It was an unlikely stroke of irony that an electrical fire trapped and killed the Kotniks in the upper hallway area of their house on the fifth anniversary of moving in. The papers spoke of the tragedy with concern and genuine loss, reflecting the place the Kotnik family held in the community. Even a quote from Rev. Hammond Coe, the local Congregational Church pastor who eulogized the family in his sanctuary to a packed out crowd of mourners, appeared. He said, *"It is horrible the death that fell upon this dear and fine family. Yet, in their deaths, they sought the grasp of loving arms and, huddled together, trapped in their home, found solace in the embrace of each other, even as God embraced them."*

Maren was especially taken by the account in the paper and had the entire article photocopied. Before returning home, she stopped by a frame shop and selected a mat and frame for the article and accompanying picture.

That evening another storm swept through town. She and Paul sat in the hall, this time hoping for the bursts of light which would advance the Kotniks into their next pose. No lightning came with this storm and they were comfortable just to sit in silence, thinking of the Kotniks.

Before dawn that same night, another brief lightning storm came into the area. Paul and Maren saw the Kotniks again, their backs turned to the bedroom and crouching together midway to slipping to the floor. Their attention was upon the stairs, where the flames were apparently crawling to the floor above. Nothing other than the family was visible. But the family - terrified, realizing that death was soon to come - was together in that locked moment. Arms entwined and heads together. Paul and Maren Fishell wept as the storm faded.

It was not long before the final appearance was made by the Kotnik family in the upper hall. Before the last entry of this mysterious slide show of the Kotnik ghosts, both Paul and Maren spent time discovering the rest of the story.

The fire which killed the Kotniks was caused by an electrical blaze within the walls. Wires caught fire in a space in the wall just at the top of the stairway which led to the second floor. One fire marshal felt that the raging lightning storm, which was in full force outside of the house, caused some sufficient effect upon the circuitry of the home which somehow ignited into fire. Perhaps lightning struck the home, or some back surge of power hit the aging wiring during a close burst. Whatever the reason, the fire exploded into the stairway as the Kotniks were attempting to descend to safety. Mr. Kotnik had called the fire department before gathering his family, but all efforts were too late and they died in the hallway, their backs against the wall facing the flames. The fire department confined the conflagration and held strong hopes of saving the family. The gruesome discovery was etched into the memories of each fire fighter who worked so bravely and diligently to rescue the family. The only thing saved was the house, which was repaired and settled as estate by the parents of Mrs. Kotnik. That was four occupancies prior to the Fishells purchase of the home.

The final frame of the progressive account of the burning of the Kotnik family came on a quiet night when the Fishells retired with no suspicion of a storm creeping into Paw Paw. When the thunder awoke the household, they each slipped quietly, almost reverently, into the hall and knelt together alongside the Kotniks. This last pose was of a family, dying from smoke and heat, yet locked in an embrace of eternal love. There was no fear in the last moments, only a visible appreciation of being together at the last. As the lightning faded, so did the Kotniks.

And newly added in the hallway hung the matted and framed memorial to the Kotnik family that Maren had created from the news clipping of the fatal fire. A reminder of the delicacy of life and that death, while always certain, can be tamed and controlled to submit to the power of love.

The Burning Barn

Mary Elaine was nearly in the house before she realized that her husband had not come to the back deck with her.

Moving the inches of dry snow on the picnic table with the blue plastic bags that contained a few groceries, she set the bags down. With curiosity she turned and followed the short driveway back around to where the truck was parked. She was going to tease him about how she had talked on and on, thinking he was right with her, only to discover she was talking to the air. And, since she had been discussing ideas for her birthday and their 15th anniversary, which were only a day apart, she'd just have to recite the list over again from the beginning.

However, her words were choked dead in her throat when she saw where he was looking. Standing in the "V" between the truck cab and the open door, her man, Bobby Jim Jones, was gaping again at the space in the back yard where the old barn used to stand some 50 years ago. This could only mean one thing. He was having one of his "visions" again. A chill swept through her that was not to be confused with the freezing winter air that covered their 30 acre farm. The ice in her spine was due to spooks, not the 20 degree temperature.

Bob and Mary Elaine Jones bought the old Gladish farm from its last owner a couple of years ago using both of their pensions, his retirement, and the remainder of the estate left to her when her first husband and only son died on a fishing trip to Nova Scotia. It was a tidy sum of money and, when linked to the selling of their house, which had been Bob's "bachelor pad" before they married, they had plenty "cash money" to pay for the property free and clear. It seemed timely that the previous owners seemed anxious to unload it quickly. Bob, being naturally suspicious, inspected the place as though searching for a bee in his briefs. He combed every inch of the land, house, and out-buildings like a gold prospector. Then he carefully copied and read just about every written record of the place available in the court house and county library. For such a deal he figured there was a toxic dump, government restriction, or space alien colony hidden somewhere in the fine print. Nothing ever turned up, so they bought it.

Gladish Farm was named over a century ago by the original farm-ers of the land and featured deep myrtle which grew along the pine tree lines which encircled the property. Mary Elaine was entertaining the idea of renaming the farm Myrtle Farm to emphasize the beautiful ground cover. When the farm was first developed it was a 200 acre farm that doglegged to the rear of Paw Paw Lake. In the early days, it was a block of land between Music and Bell streets a few miles out of Chagrin Falls, in what was then Russell Township. Over the years, blocks of land were sold off to housing projects, a horse farm, and to other farmers. Yet the original farm house, barn, out buildings and 30 acres remained intact to preserve the historicity of the farm. It was one of the only continuously producing farms in the entire valley area, which made it special. Both wanted to be part of something that still contributed. Mary Elaine and Bob bought this place to live out their years together. They were quite happy and very close, in spite of the fact that they had no family remaining. Hers had died, and he had never been married before. He often told Mary Elaine he had no better of-fers until she became available.

The space upon which the barn had once stood, the very area con-suming all of Bob's attention as he stood leaning against his truck door, now housed their compost pile. Other than the heaps of rotting grass clippings, kitchen cast offs, and other natural fertilizers, it was just an expanse of deep snow between the still fruitful apple orchard, now deep in winter's sleep, and the chicken house-turned-mower building. Yet, Mary Elaine knew that to Bob's eyes the barn was again standing erect and large as it had a half century ago.

The barn had burned in the 1930's shrouded in great mystery. Some of the family then living on the farm had perished, as had the horses and pet lambs which were housed in the barn. It simply burned to the ground one late spring afternoon with no evidence as to reason or cause.

It had been a sturdy, healthy structure; well maintained and honored for the important work it did on the farm. The owners at the time were the second and third generations of the family who had established the farm in the last century. They were hard working farmers with a sense of the flow of life involving land, crops, animals, and people. Farming was one way they completed their circle with their world - giving and receiving.

While Mary Elaine drew to mind the pictures of the barn which still hung within the farm office in the house, she knew Bob was "seeing" quite a different view of the barn. Her thoughts held sepia tones, black and whites, and an amateur painting. His, according to his descriptions, was a clear view of the barn as though it had never burned. And, in truth, if his descriptions were to be believed, he was seeing the barn stand there, as a ghost.

"I'm goin' in, Mary Elaine." He said as he shut his truck door. "You still don't see it, do ya." It was a statement, not a question. He could read in her face that the barn was invisible to her.

Clutching his arm, she asked, "Is it still burning, Bob?" She knew it was always burning when he saw it. He nodded, moving toward the compost pile. She let go and covered her mouth with her trembling hands. It was just too incredible to comprehend.

Bob shoved his hand into his pockets a bit too deeply as if demonstrating to the barn, that he was frightened but determined. As his feet crunched through the half foot cover of crusty white, he could not help but review the progressive history of his visions of the burning barn.

From the outside the barn was always on fire, always empty of animal and human. Strangely, upon entering the blazing building, the barn was never aflame. It was a normal, working farm building and he could hear lots of sounds. Once across the threshold, the massive doors were always open to the growing spring. He would get a blast of sunshine from the open doors of the haymow which let in the afternoon sun. The huge sliding doors at the far end of the barn were always wide open to greening pastures. The animals were making content eating or resting sounds. A cat was purring loudly in a hidden corner. And in the haymow, voices could be heard whispering with an occasional giggle.

This was the scene that always greeted him as he stepped through the door of the barn no matter what season or hour. The silently burning, tightly closed structure was so different after he crossed the threshold, passing not through a doorway, but through the door itself. It seemed to him like some crazy special effect straight from a high-budget Sci-Fi movie. He had figured out over time, when the barn decided to show itself, that somehow time was passing in two different streams. At least, that's what it seemed like. The fiery conflagration was the end of the story. The details inside were leading up to the fire. Today, as he already knew, he would take the story line a step further. *Maybe to the last scene this time,* he silently prayed.

Bob Jones was not an imaginative man. His tastes ran to hunting and fishing and visiting church friends with Mary Elaine, although he almost never attended church. He liked reruns of old TV westerns, like *Gunsmoke, Cheyenne* and *The High Chaparral.* He liked gardening and loved the bit of farming Mary Elaine and he did together. He was partial to volunteering at "do something, make something" missions like Habitat for Humanity. These were the simple expressions of culture which fit this honest and simple man. He had all he wanted or needed from life and had no notion as to why he was picked to figure out this barn's mystery.

Yet, Bob was a man not afraid to face a task. He could be trusted to complete whatever it was he undertook. With that same determination, he again stepped through the cold, ghostly surface of the burning barn into its bright and warm interior world. Stepping through, he vanished out of Mary Elaine's sight. Beyond his hearing, she once again let a small wail of fear escape her lips.

The first thing Bob noticed today was that the purring cat was accompanied by several smaller purrs. Immediately he knew that the purring cat was nursing a batch of new kittens, all equally contented with the connection of mother to offspring. Slowly walking down the center of the barn's hard packed dirt floor, he noted again the equipment and tools all neatly lined up in vacant animal stalls. He leaned over to closely inspect the plate describing the model of the Ford tractor parked in the stall. From memory, he confirmed it as a model made in America in the late 1930's. Here it was about six years old. In reality, it was over 70 years old and a collector's dream.

Slowly backing out of the stall, amid contented neighs, and a troubled "baa," he moved closer to the haymow to again eavesdrop on the couple upstairs as they spoke of their feelings after their lovemaking. Over the months, he had deduced that the woman was the farm owner's wife. The gent was the full time, live-in "man," as they were called in those days. Full time, live-in, and apparently surrogate sex partner for the philandering wife. He always sensed he was drawing closer with each encounter to the moments before the origin of the fire. Haunting him was the question if the fire was accident or intentional. And, if intentional, set by whom? He had come to wonder if the woman set the blaze in response to the farm hand's plea that she run away with him. Maybe not for murder, but maybe for a diversion. Or was it the man? Did he set the fire as a punishment for her reluctance and hesitation to leave her husband for him? Just recently, Bob began to wonder if a third person caused the fire, or an accident with one of the animals?

The remarkable effect of this "in the barn" vision was that while absent of living creatures, it reflected their actions by the shifting and movements of the inanimate. Hay filtered through the crack of the haymow as the lovers romped. Dust rose in little puffs along the dividers of the stalls as unseen tails presumably swayed away unseen flies. The occasional bumping of one of the sheep against the railing of their containment caused a shovel to slide into a corner. A makeshift plastic door would rise and fall as the sheep occasionally passed to the pasture. It was in tracking these effects from the invisible agents causing them that drew Bob's attention to the lantern which hung, lit, on one of the main vertical supports of the barn's structure, right next to the ladder which reached to the haymow.

Had this lantern been left alight and unnoticed from the past evening? Had someone lit it in the morning during chores and forgotten it? Or, had it been lit by one of the unviewed couple still amid groans of pleasure in the loft? Intuitively, Bob knew that the answer to the barn's demise lay in the answer of this single question.

While researching the farm before purchasing it, Bob had learned that the burning of the barn was unsolved. All of the animals had been killed. And so had the farmer's wife and his hired man. The farmer himself had been in town on an errand. It was not until after the barn had collapsed, the paper reported, that he discovered his wife and hand were also in the barn. No speculation had been publically given as to what the two might have been doing in the barn in the middle of a work day. None was needed.

Bob was brought back to the matters at hand when a new voice rose into the rafters of the barn from the outside. It was a third human voice, calling from beyond the north sliding door of the barn, which faced the house. Bob was just under the haymow which lined the south and east walls above the stable area. At the man's call a dog, apparently almost under where Bob was standing, began barking happily as it dashed to the front door. Bob nearly passed out at the deep bark of the farm dog. He noted with fascination the pebbles and clods of dirt that its running paws shot off behind as it happily sprint toward the calling voice.

From above came hard whispers and the unmistakable sounds of clothing being quickly thrown on. The woman let out a sob of fear. Looking up, Bob could see hay falling over the edge of the loft in clumps. The ladder creaked as someone scurried down, the rungs slightly bending from the weight. Dust rose as two impressions of a man's feet appeared at the base of the ladder. As second avalanche of hay came through the uprights of the ladder as the woman descended. She was nearly wheezing in fear.

From outside the voice called once again into the spring air. Movement on the ladder stopped dead.

"Eugene! Where in blazes are you, man? Why aren't you plowing the back corn field?"

Only silence followed.

Mumbling to himself the farmer said, "I suppose that tractor is acting up again. 'Gene ain't one to dodge work."

Bob realized how trusting the farmer was of his wife and hand. *He doesn't know*, thought Bob.

From the ladder the woman gasped. The next sound was of fabric tearing, which was followed by the lantern falling and crashing on the hard packed dirt and gravel of the barn floor. The flames seemed to shoot from the dry hay; the last remaining stock of last fall's cut. A form outlined by the fire appeared before Bob. The kerosene had splashed the man and set his clothing on fire. As he shrieked and fell to attempt to extinguish the flames, the woman wailed a prayer to God. As the man rolled and banged into stalls, barn posts, tools, and the thin layer of fallen hay, he left a trail of flame. In seconds, the entire section was consumed in burning red and yellow fire.

The woman had apparently forgotten her need for secrecy and she could be heard hitting the flames on the farmhand with her bare hands. Her outline began to be shaped by fire.

Bob heard a terrified *Oh my God!* From behind himself and turned to see who was speaking. In the doorway, he could see a brownish figure, a silhouette of a tall man, framed by the sunlight which flowed into the barn from behind. The figure looked ready to leap and assist, then, he hesitated seeing his wife and worker as they wrestled the flames which were growing, fed on hay and flesh. The farmer slowly turned and shortly the sound of a truck firing up and pulling away competed with the growing noise of the flames.

It was not murder, in the truest sense. Yet, from some recess of memory, Bob flashed on a sentence from a Communion prayer he heard so often as a child. Something about asking for God to forgive us of the sins we have done but to also forgive the sins we have committed from deeds left undone. The sin of omission.

As he passed from the late spring of the barn and into the hard winter of his reality and the waiting arms of his dear Mary Elaine, Bob's questions were answered. He knew the barn would not burn before him ever again. Just as he knew it was the barn, and not the people or animals, that needed the story of its death to be known by someone.

May it rest in peace.

Shimmer

It began late one September afternoon as Annie let a moving light distract her attention from the florescent orange bobber that was all too still upon the placid surface of the murky waters of Paw Paw Lake. She had been "willing" a fish to strike the baited hook and bring some action to her rod and reel. She knew that fishing at 4:30 on a hot, late summer afternoon carried few guarantees of a catch or even a curiosity strike. Still, she needed to extend summer as long as possible into her current school year. Classrooms forgotten for the day, she came to the lake every afternoon as a physical denial that school and the coloring of autumn leaves were sapping her energies and passions.

As she fished, her peripheral vision picked up on what she would soon refer to as "the shimmer." As she stared at the lifeless bobber, off to her right and in the path that sharply divided the lake from a thick grove of pines, she noted a movement similar to the heat waves that rise off of a car during summer's hottest days. It was that familiar heat wave that indicated the baking reflection of undeterred solar energy broiling the world below.

As she turned her head to witness the distracting movement with full vision it seemed to disappear. Shrugging, Annie looked again at the hopeless bobber and smiled as she reflected on the Zen-like wisdom of the bumper stickers which she had proudly placed in the center of her bedroom door, on her Trapper Keeper, and under the lid of her tackle box – "A bad day fishing is better than any day at work." With a marker she had scrawled "school" over the word "work" on each sticker.

The movement reoccurred and Annie reflexively regarded the area once again only to see nothing. A slight chill brushed within her stomach. *Now I'm seeing things* she thought with a sigh. Yet, she knew she was seeing something. She was not the type to doubt in resignation to what seemed to be fact or the opinion of the rest of the world. With self-assured certainty, she knew that whatever it was would only become visible if not examined directly. It was sort of like straining to see something in the dark. You couldn't look dead on.

With fishing long departed from her attention, Annie returned an unseeing stare toward the orange bobber, still motionless, and set to work at seeing something she could not truly see. The strain to find the shimmer moistened her eyes with tears. She blinked the tears of eyestrain away, thinking of them as eye sweat from exertion, and relaxed her gaze.

She saw the shimmering immediately. She let her eyes drift across the lake surface, looking back and forth, up, down, trying every angle to determine where the shimmering might become clearer in her side vision. A few feet to the right of her bobber, shortening the distance between her gaze and the shimmer, the movement of heat took the form of a person, a woman.

In the instinct of terror, Annie dropped her fishing pole and leapt to her feet, hands up to defend herself if that became necessary. In horror she looked directly into the shimmering female. There was no one there.

In the stillness of the warm afternoon, her now-heightened senses gathered each detail and scrap of motion and sound. It was as though all life had ceased, trapped in a still photograph. Heart racing and ears abuzz with panic, she shook her shoulder length hair in frenzy, scouring the spot of the shimmer that had only moments before been inhabited by the woman. Nothing was there that should not be there. The background of pines, the tall, browning grasses and weeds, beer cans and a locking pole for canoes, some rotting branches – only what could be expected.

She gathered her courage and moved cautiously toward the spot looking for the imprint of a shoe or bare foot in the soft earth and grasses – there was no sign of person or presence. Looking closely into the woods she saw nothing to indicate escape. Not a branch swayed. No weed was bent or rocking. Coldness encompassed her in stark opposition to the heat of the afternoon. Her soul felt frozen in ways not unlike the deep winters she experienced in this snow belt of Ohio. She felt, for the first time in her young life, the touch of something beyond the realm of the physical world.

Quickly gathering her fishing gear in an attempt to settle down, she hurried along the path and up the incline toward her house. She told herself it was getting late and she had lots of math homework to tackle.

Annie McAllister was one half of a set of 15-year-old twins born to John and Becky McAllister. Her identical sis, the other expression of the same egg was Kathy. Kathy watched her sister scurry up the path and sensed that something was not quite right. Annie's posture and stride said that something had alarmed her. Now, her own respiration deepened and she began to sweat around her collar as she always did when the two shared feelings that seemed to be theirs as twins. She headed to the garage to intercept Annie, holding the back door open for her.

Dropping her tackle box alongside of their "tool bench," Annie knew that Kathy felt her distress. "Up to our room," Annie commanded, leading off through the kitchen. Kathy followed in silence, opening her senses to analyze Annie's sudden distress. This was more, much more, than hating school or not catching fish.

These twins could not have been more different in attitude, appearance and appetites. Where Annie was more Tom boyish, Kathy was akin to Barbie. Annie was head strong, athletic and bold. While Kathy was also appropriately athletic, she was diplomatic and leaned toward "girlish" sports like ballet. Quite unlike Annie, Kathy tended to give thought before blurting out a response.

While very different in worldview and demeanor, the twins shared many sensory similarities and perceptions on an emotional level — especially when one felt some threat. This almost shared consciousness was what kept the girls close even as their paths in life continued to separate. Thus, the shared room in a four-bedroom house that only held mom, dad and the twins. It was this link that served as a prelude to Annie's description of what she saw.

Kathy listened carefully as Annie spoke. She believed her sister, not because her details were so clear or her story so compelling, but because of her knotted stomach and machine gun heartbeat. Mystically to their family doctor, Dr. Mary Post, when examined for sports physicals, the girls always had precisely the same pulse rate and blood pressure readings. Dr. Post always felt that this would make for a fascinating scientific study for twins, but lacked the motivation to figure out how to do such a study. It was this shared bodily response that gave Kathy the inside confirmation of Annie's account. Kathy was convinced that Annie saw what she said she saw.

Huddled among the mass of pillows that adorned the floor between their beds, the space they shared whenever they talked seriously, they discussed the phenomena, as Kathy liked calling it, at great length. Kathy sought details, looking for clarity or other explanations for Annie's strange experience. Even while Kathy asked questions, both girls knew neither had any doubt.

Using patience forged through many such interrogations by her sister, Annie dutifully jumped through the hoops and counterpoints that Kathy put forth. In the end, the best explanation for Kathy was that Annie had witnessed a reflection of light from some unconsidered source. Fighting a smirk, Annie dared Kathy to accompany her to the lake for a look-see.

The sojourn began as a nerve racking retracing of her steps for Annie, fearful of what she might see. In the end she was only disappointed. Try as she might, she could not re-engage the specter. Kathy saw this as confirmation to her light reflection theory (*A car or plane,*

Annie. That's what it was. Now it's long gone. You just saw light.) Discouraged, a bit embarrassed, but never defeated, Annie bit the bitter pill and returned home with her twin, trying to overlook the certainty that Kathy held of solving the mystery.

Annie was quiet throughout the evening. She surprised her mother by sitting in front of, but not watching, a game that would put the Indians in the playoffs. It was late in the eighth and the Tribe was trailing. Usually this was when Annie blocked the TV from other viewers as she started her own personal rally with the Tribe's bullpen. Tonight, however, she gazed through the screen into some inner world. Her mother casually felt her forehead for a fever, inquiring as to how Annie felt.

"I'm ok," she answered, "Just tired I guess."

Unbelievably, Annie went off to bed without even watching the Tribe rally for a win in the ninth. Becky was a touch worried. The Indians had become a family tradition since before the 1995 season that brought strong baseball back to Cleveland and an astonishing sell out record of 455 consecutive home stand sellouts. For "Pop" McAllister, the Indians were his connection with "the three ladies" as he referred to Bets and the twins. Enthusiastically they had supported the team from famine to the heights of their second half of the 1990's reign of near glory. The only TV program that could draw the family away from the dining table was a Tribe game. No "how was your day" conversation and no slurping and smacking corrections. Only coaching from the couch by Pop and cheers from the three ladies. As good Christians, Jesus was King, but the Indians were Kong.

All of this understood, leaving an Indians game unwatched and unfinished was somewhat taboo. Certainly it was unheard of in the McAllister home. Becky was concerned and glanced at her husband to get his read on it. However, he didn't even notice when Kathy departed after her sister, gesturing to her mother that it was OK and she should remain seated. Both girls again occupied the pillows between their beds in their room.

"You hate it when I'm right" Kathy began chiding in reference to her view that the shimmering was a reflection.

"Nope, I hate it when you're stupid. I've never experienced you being right," her sister shot back.

"Ooh, a sucker punch. But facts is facts, twinny. Reflections – not ghosts."

Annie removed her t-shirt and all but tore off her bra. "I hate these things" she muttered as she itched along the half circles beneath her young breasts.

"Which things? Boobs or bras?" Kathy continued in her mocking.

Wanting to blurt out "Boobs!" Annie chose to ignore her sister and put on her boxers and a clean sleep shirt. Uncharacteristically, she was avoiding the fray with Kathy. Without some alternative explanation, reasonable or otherwise, she had no ammunition for dispute. Yet, inside, it just galled her. She knew what she had seen and it was not the sun bouncing off of the windshield of a Jeep Cherokee. The "ghost," which is what she supposed it was, had been as real as a ghost could be. If ghosts can be real. Lacking proof or alternative ideas, she remained silent. Better to sizzle in silence than to give Kathy more material for ridicule.

At 2:15 that morning, Annie knelt next to Kathy amid the sea of pillows and clothes that littered the aisle between their beds and flicked on Kathy's light. She shook Kathy into semi-wakefulness.

"Kath," whispered Annie hoping not to wake their light sleeping mom, "I did see it and I have proof."

"Get off me," moaned Kathy into her pillow.

"Kath, I have proof that I saw something, a ghost maybe. Wake up!"

Pushing Annie's clutching hand aside; Kathy leaned up on her elbow to squint at the red glowing numbers on the clock in her headboard bookshelf.

"2:15? You are such a pig." She rolled back into her covers.

"Shush." Annie hissed as she moved her face to Kathy's ear. "I know that I saw something and you do too. You felt it when I ran up the yard yesterday. And when I told you about it, I'll just bet your heart was pounding too. Just like mine was. We always feel each other's disasters and you felt mine, didn't you?"

"You wake me up for that?" asked Kathy with growing anger. "You lame-o. I told you, you saw something that spooked you, but it was only a reflection, not a ghost. You glimpsed it, believed it, freaked out and ran. I must have felt your fear of being stupid, not of some monster. Now leave me alone or I'll talk so Mom can hear us."

"Listen to me, Kath." Annie's intensity struck Kathy with a tinge of fear. "We know each other way too well for me to believe that you think I'm freaked out because I saw a flash of light in the bushes. Don't think Kath, feel."

New chills itched along Kathy's vertebrae. Inside she backed down and felt. Annie was right. Somehow. Quietly, in surrender to the notion that her sister had seen something supernatural, she said, "OK, Go away and I'll sleep on it – that's the best I can do at this hour."

But she slept very little.

As the sisters worked out the possibilities of the specter on the school bus ride to and from school, they determined a couple of things. The decided that their best course was to re-enact what Annie had done the previous day. Sit quietly, fish, and wait. Kathy was not much of a fisher-girl, but she knew how and figured she could go through the motions. Annie agreed that this might work and, skipping their snack, they checked in with their mom and quickly set up their observation at the lake.

They spoke very little. Both girls nervously continued glancing into the area where Annie's original encounter had occurred. They grew anxious as the four o'clock hour pressed on. Annie silently suspected that the time had some relationship to the appearance. Nervously, she hoped that she was wrong. As 4:30 grew closer, she began to sense a change in the air, the lines around the leaves and grass sharpening. The lake seemed clearer, more defined somehow. She suddenly wanted to leave and to not be right – even if it meant sucking up to Kathy.

With eyes darting from bobber to grove to the surrounding area to Kathy and back again, Annie noticed that Kathy was statue-like in her posture, sitting totally still. Her bobber took a dip beneath the water's surface; Kathy remained still, unnoticing. It began to slowly move toward the shore and then more swiftly out into the lake. Kathy let the line run out, not pulling back to set the hook. Annie grabbed the reel from Kathy's hands, but the bait and fish were gone. The bobber stilled once again. In irritation, Annie turned to Kathy, but found her sister occupied in other ways, her body turned from Annie toward the woods. Her hands slack, mouth drooping. A gurgle of fear and increased, rapid breathing filling her lungs. Standing between Annie and the tree area of the shimmering, Kathy blocked Annie's view of whatever it was that caused such fear. Annie knew without seeing that Kathy was becoming a believer. She slowly stepped from behind her sister and again watched the movement of the shimmer, still unclear to the girls.

"Kath, look back toward the bobbers and watch the light in your side vision" Annie whispered.

Kathy stood in frozen terror. She could not see the woman, but she knew that the light was not a reflection of anything made by humans. It had a strange cast and quiver. It pulsated and seemed to have a motion of flow, not like a flashlight being waved from side-to-side, but like sunlight upon the surface of a fast flowing river. The light trembled and waned, slipping towards the direction of the lake.

Watching directly as Kathy did, Annie noticed today that the light did not move off of the surfaces of the trees and bushes behind it, but moved as if it were its own shape and form. Like a candle moving in a vast open space, the light would be strong but lacking a reflecting surface, it would stand on its own. This light was much the same. It was its own light and not given to illuminate anything.

"Look away from it and you'll see the lady" Annie again whispered to her sister.

Instead, Kathy bolted toward home, never looking back or calling out. With the speed of terror, she quickly disappeared up the hill to their house.

Annie could not join her in fleeing. The fact that this existed was disturbing enough. That it was measured and predictable was too much for her to ignore. She was filled with fear but determined to figure this out.

Uneasily, she turned and the image of a woman was defined again, dressed in a long skirt of another time. Annie noted that the woman was not beautiful, but she looked to be determined and confident. Her movement was simple. She slowly proceeded toward the lake, not twenty feet from where Annie stood.

By this time the day before, Annie had cleared the scene. Today she lingered, itching to run but resolute.

The ghost, for certainly that is what it was, slowly advanced toward the water's edge and, in perfect relation to her advancement, began to fade, completely disappearing before reaching the water.

Annie released the breath she had held so long and slumped to the ground in exhaustion, which was how Kathy found her. Meekly returning from her flight of fear, she murmured that she just couldn't abandon her twin.

In silence, they sat on the warm summer grass, smelling the late summer heat and the musk of the drying plants that circled the lake. Slowly, they relaxed and began looking around them at the beauty of the golds and turning browns, still in the grasp of the last lingering greens of stalk and leaf. Annie lay back and looked toward the ghost's path from grove to lake. Kathy avoided the spot with her eyes, preferring instead to take great interest in the still bobbers from their fishing gear. Annie sniffed and offered a fake cough.

"What can I say," she softly began, "when I'm right, I'm right."

"Nice job at hooking my fish while I died a thousand deaths with that ghost," Kathy nagged.

"Let's go home."

Annie stood to gather the fishing equipment, helping her sister to her feet. Slowly, silently, they returned home, dutifully hanging the rods and putting their tackle boxes on the shelf.

Days slowly turned into weeks. The girls said little of the ghost, but every day after school they would return to their post to watch the woman traverse between her starting point and the place of disappearance along the edge of the lake.

Each day it was the same event played over and over, like a favorite music video on MTV. While they never grew tired of watching the woman, they did constantly grapple with why she was there.

At night they would develop theories of her life and death. Was she locked into this world until some mystery be solved? This was Kathy's belief. Was she a carry-over from a lost time, forever destined to re-enact her brief trek? Was she a clue, or did her appearance accomplish some unknown purpose in the larger framework of nature? Annie thought that she might be one of millions of similar peeks into another realm.

Kathy decided to investigate this specter of the last century and began visiting the older neighbors of the community of fifty or so homes along their lake. Avoiding her reasons, she simply posed gathering the story of the community for a school project on the early history of the Western Reserve. She learned of farmers, of vacationers, of rich Clevelanders who purchased homes in the country for weekend getaways. Nothing was learned of the last century or the mysterious woman.

Annie was better suited to log on to the Internet for possible hints in the history of the Chagrin Valley and ghosts in general.

As summer became dominated by fall and pumpkins glowed in

their fields, their vines dark with the ruin of the first hard frost, the leaves gave up their brief displays of radiant color to pummel to the earth. This act of dying became the backdrop as the girls continued their quest. In the midst of each shortening day they made a pilgrimage to view the specter's walk to the lake.

It was Kathy who decided to attempt to contact or distract the ghost. One afternoon she boldly and spontaneously (had she thought of doing this she would have talked herself out of it), approached the ghost midway between her appearance and her coming disappearance. The ghost took no notice of Kathy.

In the days that followed, since Kathy had not disintegrated on the spot in her attempt to interrupt, the girls tried other means of gaining the ghost's attention. From standing in front of her, allowing her to pass through them (there was no sensation or exchange of inner knowledge), to throwing rocks and sticks through her, to making fun of her and spitting through her, the girls exhausted every idea of contact.

As the early November clouds began to frequently boil in preparation for carrying the snows of winter, they one day found themselves being observed after the daily visitation of the ghost. As they walked the path home, silent in the continued brooding of the ghost, they realized that they were not alone. Their mother quietly greeted them and walked back with them silently to their home where she had prepared them all a snack of hot cocoa and oatmeal raisin cookies.

Annie and Kathy were not going to introduce the topic of the ghost. Their hope was that their mother either did not or could not see the apparition and they could avoid explaining their daily trip to the lake. As they had long since abandoned the pretext of fishing, they had no good explanation for their outings.

"Mrs. Jensen is so delighted that you're studying the history of the area and the lake, Kathy." Their mother began. "She called me last night to remind you to stop by again anytime if you want to talk about it more."

Kathy dipped her cookie into her cocoa, something that all three of them knew she never did. Annie fumed at the way her sister was blowing their secret.

"The library called for you, Annie. The book on the prominent settlers of the Western Reserve that you asked them to get from the Burton library is in. Said you put a rush on it. Maybe your father will take you after dinner." Becky absently circled the mug of cocoa with her thumb as she relayed this to Annie.

Annie held her mug half way to her lips, frozen in shocked discovery. Now it was Kathy who glared at her twinny for blowing their secret.

Rising, turning her back to her girls, Mrs. McAllister looked out the kitchen window to the lake. The grove where the ghost moved was around a bend and not visible from the house.

"I call her Mrs. Hortense, after a woman I knew when I was a little girl in Pennsylvania. Mrs. Hortense wore dresses like the one the woman at the lake wears."

Sound ceased to exist in the room. Annie and Kathy could not look at their mother. Their ears rang with fear. Kathy's breath had hitched in her lungs.

"I guess I'd mostly forgotten about her in the last few years," she continued. "But I was like you at first. There every day watching her. Trying to figure out if there was something I could do to release her. Trying to decide if she was in torment. I hit the library and asked the neighbors, but I found nothing, just like you'll find nothing. But look anyway. Look as much as you like and as long as you can. Because if you don't try to figure her out, well, you'll go nuts like I did.

"I do know that she's not natural, girls. That's what I think. That's what I believe. She's dead and she should stay that way. I'm not God though, so I just tried to forget her."

She turned to them slowly, almost like she was turning in gelatin.

"When I got pregnant with the two of you, I used to take you with me to go see her. You both were always so still, so quiet in my womb. Never a kick or a turn from either of you while I watched her disappear into the lake.

"My best guess is that she just is," Becky glanced from one girl back to the other, "and for whatever reason, she walks every day from some long gone starting place to some long gone destination. And that's all there is to it. It's just too… ah, Mrs. Hortense."

Mother slowly left the room leaving her daughters to gawk at the unknown worlds unfolding in the film atop their mugs of cooling cocoa.

After all these ghosties,
I thought you might like
something different for dessert.

Salsa

She was waiting now. Waiting for whatever end was to come. She could hear them screaming and moving in the kitchen area. They were violently redoing the whole downstairs if the sounds were indicative of what she imagined in her mind.

She searched the room once again, as she had a million times in the last hours, looking for some escape, some weapon, some clue to lead her to survival. Again, no encouragement. No reprieve.

Cautiously she pulled one leg up and massaged the muscles. She adjusted her butt on the bed pillow she was using to break the hardness of the floor. Her back was pushing against the huge, thick, timber foot board of the bed; her feet cramping in pressure as they pushed the door to keep it closed. Her body was her only wedge, now thrust between door and bed, creating a hopelessly inadequate obstacle to keep the door forced closed.

If only she could get to morning.

She didn't think she could.

Signe Casey was way too excited at seeing her sister after two years of continental separation. Having spent some years in Italy to complete her art history degree, she was now home again and off to see her sister, Kate, who lived in an art colony in rural Geauga County, Ohio.

Checking her watch, Signe estimated that she was only about 40 minutes from her sister's place. Her flight had somehow arrived early into Hopkins Airport in spite of the continuous flurries that now drifted onto the windshield. "It's the tail winds." the businessman next to her had tried to explain. She might actually be able to surprise her sister if she kept the gas pedal close to the floor. She involuntarily grinned as she replayed the reunion she had hourly imagined.

Kate had consistently begged off visiting Italy. There was always some supposed reason which Signe could not overcome in plea or pressure. She knew that Kate did not fear flying, for they had often flown together as girls to visit their mom in California. Divorce had made the world larger after her mother and Juan, her former hair-dresser and now common law husband, took off to "the real world," as Juan liked to put it, which translated into a small town near Big Sur. Being busy, or ill, or on commission, or too poor did not convince Signe that Kate wasn't being a jerk. What an opportunity to stay al-most for free in one of the great arts cultures of all time. Yet, Kate had remained in her small southeastern suburb of Cleveland, unmoved.

Signe lurched ahead as the traffic thinned at the interstate lane divide that took most of the traffic north to Cleveland. The concrete artery she needed pointed due east to what she imagined as a warm, cozy farm house, aging with dignity and character. Making a mental calculation and reviewing the picture of the map in her head, as de-scribed by her sister over and over again, she thought she might actu-ally be there an hour or so before expected. Snow seemed to hold no delay. With anticipation she placed her hand on the package of Italian souvenirs and art books occupying the seat next to her. She would gift her sister with love, stories and new treasures.

Slipping into the kind of zone one finds late at night when driving on open highway, Signe settled into the rest of her trip.

As she pulled into the twisting driveway, Signe glanced at her watch again, not seeing the glowing numbers on the face. She slid a bit as she maneuvered her car between the high florescent red snow stakes that marked the driveway for the snow plow guy. He obviously had not come yet as she could see no break in the whiteness of the cold carpet of pushed snow. She relished the fact that she had indeed beaten the clock, but it was all for naught in comparison to joy the next minutes would bring. Kate's face filled her mind - large blue eyes, open smile, that naughty laugh which only Signe understood. But mostly, her flawless complexion and naturally rouged cheeks which only hinted of the energy and life that played within.

Stepping out of the car, which she brought to a halt near the front door of the house, she flashed on how truthful her sister had described the huge volumes of snow which so often fell in this part of northeastern Ohio. The "Lake Effect" was what Kate called it. Some meteorological phenomenon of Lake Erie which dumped feet of snow in this three county corner of Ohio while the rest of the state only experienced a couple of inches. Her feet disappeared into what must have been a foot and a half of fluffy white still stacking up inches. She wondered why the drive hadn't been plowed?

Carving a path as she walked, Signe made her way to the front door, climbing the steps onto the front porch. The steps creaked in muffled warning bearing the weight of the snow and her frame. The stoop had not been shoveled. She kicked the snow in happiness and then wondered if the porch was safe. Oh well, she was there now. Might as well let it rip.

As she raised her hand to knock, she heard the distressing sounds of an argument in which two voices competed for the position of being heard. Their din was unintelligible, but their emotion was as plain as the raised fist she held before her face, frozen in the arc of the first knock. She gave pause, unsure. Perhaps this was not the right house after all.

When she heard her name linked with profanity, the joy of her visit, long anticipated, leaked from her like the air from a pierced tire of a child's bike. As if attached to the seeping of her excitement and the promise of a visit with her only sibling, her raised fist wilted to her side. She listened, turning her head and moving an ear closer to the door.

"It's just like you to bring people here." A voice both gruff and feminine shouted. "What about us and our lives? Ever think of us? What about our ..." She was interrupted by the unmistakable voice of Kate as her response cut off whatever it was the she-cow was going to use as leverage.

"There is no debate here. She is my sister and she is coming. You may have an opinion, but you and the others have no say in this. She will be here. She is staying two days. You can maintain on..." She could not understand the last word. It sounded like she said *salsa*.

What could rhyme with salsa that would be something one would use to maintain? Actually, did anything rhyme with salsa? Obviously not anything that made sense.

As the fighting continued, although with less ferocity after Kate's retort, Signe took a few uncertain steps back from the front door and moved to take in what she could of the house and grounds. She knew it would be wise to let them conclude and "tidy up" the matter before barging in. She was, after all, quite early. She also knew that nothing was going to dissuade her from seeing her sister - be it the snow, the expense, or some mean broad with an unpleasant voice. Kate would square things around. She'd just give them a few.

In the darkness Signe could see very little, but enough to make out at least two small barns, a snow covered truck, and a garage near the side door. The house was large as it blotted out its shape against the back drop of deep and falling snow. A little light glowed as it illuminated the inside of the pulled shades at every window, but no light darted furtively from under the window covers. Obviously the tightness of the coverings was to insure that as much heat remained inside as possible. These old farms were notoriously hard to heat.

The house was a standard two story, turn of the century farm house with clap board siding and a tall attic. Ornamental, flying gables extended at the peaks. The enclosed front porch was in disrepair, its screens rusted and torn, but it was of the classic porch design that wrapped around the house to face the side yard. She imagined that the house needed a coat of paint, but was not sure in the darkness. It appeared sturdy.

Moving back toward her car she noted that hers were the only tracks in the snow. She reasoned that either the colony inside was made up of home bodies, or the snow was just from today. According to Kate, it could snow a foot in a couple of hours - and it often did, as it seemed to be doing now. It seemed reasonable that those inside had stayed home for the day. Knowing that Kate was never long in any one place, Signe had some difficulty imagining her not going out a half dozen times in a day. She was a roamer, even if only from room to room or from home to town.

Leaning against her car, she listened deeply into the quiet of the night. It sounded as though the fighting was over. The silence of the snow filled night was matched by the silence now coming from the house. She loved how snow seemed to be the ultimate sound absorber. She pictured the cow-woman in her room, tending her wounds. No one could keep Kate and Signe apart. They had endured too much pain together in childhood. Such bonds were strong and eternal.

Feigning that she just arrived, although she had now been there for over 20 minutes, Kate opened her car door, slammed it, and went a second time to the front porch, ascending the steps carefully. She made a production of opening the aluminum screen door, jiggling it for the racket they were so famous for, and rapped sharply on the windowless wooded door. The quiet house somehow became even more silent.

Minutes passed. She banged again, assuming that the crew had retired upstairs to make final preparations for the guest both welcome and unwelcome. The cold was beginning to penetrate her parka and she suddenly fell to a deep shiver.

Raising her fist to again attack the door, she jumped as the voice behind her spoke her name. Whipping around, amazed that anyone could be so silent, she let her body sag against the door and instinctively pulled the storm door to her body in shield-like protection.

Before her, standing on the first step, was a tall woman with long, light hair. She wore no coat and was clothed in a calf length "earth mother" dress. She had on ankle booties, but that was all in terms of winter protection.

She spoke again, "You must be Katie's little sister. It is Signe, isn't it?"

Allowing the storm door to open away from her, but increasing her grip, she nodded that she was. What was on this woman's face? Her mouth was ringed with some residue of food. Like a chocolate milk mustache gone crazy.

"Yes," She began in a dubious whisper, "I've come to visit Kate. She's expecting me." She thought how defensively that sounded.

"We don't use this door much. Come in through the side door." She turned without a glance and led the way back toward Signe's rented car. She spoke not another word at the side door, yet turned to hold it open for Signe.

Signe climbed the steps which led into a tiny mud room that fed into a large kitchen. Around an ancient, light yellow enameled table showing plenty of chips in its finish, sitting in 50's vintage red vinyl padded chairs with discolored white piping, were four other women. Oblivious to Signe's appearance, the continued to hover over a large bowl of what appeared to be chunked green peppers and tomatoes, and eat. Most used taco chips, but one woman was simply scooping with her fingers and stuffing the dripping concoction into her mouth. The room smelled of Mexican spices.

The woman behind her placed a hand at her back to propel her into the room. As she heard the door behind her close, the four sets of eyes rose in unison to examine her. The staring eyes were cold and somehow fierce. Almost as one they turned back to the bowl and their eating, as if forcing themselves not to acknowledge her. Signe lost some of her bravado and wished she had not made the long trip for what she had thought would be a wonderful reunion with her sis.

As if on cue, Kate flowed into the kitchen. Her arms were already up and open, her face cut with a smile of depth and unbridled rapture. Ignoring the others, she gathered her sister into her arms, deeply holding her, and, in silence, clutched her as a lover. Signe melted into the strong embrace.

When she opened her eyes, moments later, the five women were all watching. The one who found her outside unconsciously wiped her sleeve across her mouth, smearing the red sauce from her mouth to her cheek.

Kate loosened her hold and held her sister at arm's length. Throwing her head back, she laughed.

"Sigie," she said, "you have the look of an immortal beauty. Only you could travel the world and become even younger. It must be that Italian wine." And, in that greeting, the dam of reservation and anxiety broke into a flood of sisterly catching up which lasted for hours, in spite of the non-participation of the others, who remained unintroduced.

It was pushing morning when Kate finally showed a contented and happy Signe to her room. Alone in the small cubicle adorned only with a bed and a dresser, she turned out the light and peeked through the side of the pulled shade. The small part of the yard she could see was empty and unbroken. Snow still fell, huge and fat, against the storm window. Kate had the thought that it was almost like a caterpillar being imprisoned in the furry cage of its own making. In exhaustion, she sank into the bed and dreamed of endless snow.

Signe wakened in the late morning for no apparent reason. She mentally reviewed the glorious reunion with contentment. Pushing from the mattress she was reminded of her sister's old saying, "You can sleep anytime. But you can only eat breakfast in the morning." Slipping into her jeans and a ski sweater, she became aware that she was hungry and ready for round two of the catch-up fest.

Arriving in the kitchen, Signe was surprised to find it empty.

She knew that at least six people, all women it seemed thus far, were probably at home. Scanning the driveway through the side door window, she noted that her car was covered with snow and no vehicles had troubled the snow. Her path of last evening was filled and now but a memory.

With some aggravation, she cleared the table of empty bowls. She still smelled the sharp scent of the mixture and spices, but the bowls were clean, as if licked. Putting the dirty dishes in the sink, she wiped the table and searched for a tea pot and coffee. Strangely, there was none of either. The cupboards were the proverbial bare, except for a few items in the refrigerator and one shelf of various cans of food. Spying a small pantry on the wall near what were probably the basement stairs, she opened it for her first shock of the day.

The seven identical shelves were filled, from the front to back, with jars of Mexican salsa. And nothing else.

Bewildered, she closed the pantry doors and sat at the kitchen table. They only ate salsa?

After a time, Signe rose to root through the other shelf of canned goods she had discovered. Pushing aside cans of tuna, and beans, and ready-made pasta, she found a small jar of instant coffee. Saved, she put water in a small, mostly clean pan and set it to boil on the ancient electric stove. She felt some relief when the circle of elements began to glow red. For the lack of other diversions, she watched and waited for the water to boil.

Late morning slipped into early afternoon, which gave way to mid-afternoon. Signe could not believe she was alone in the house. Her upbringing did not permit her to peek into the closed doors which lined the upper halls like stacked dominoes painted white. She knew that Kate was in one of the rooms, but would hazard no quick glimpse. To kill time she retrieved and unpacked her sparse luggage. These characters did not even have a TV or radio. If there was a phone, it must be in a room somewhere.

By late afternoon, as the dimming light of day drained from the sky in that winter woolen gray, she decided to take her destiny into her hands and go get some food. Salsa was not going to make it.

Winter in this part of Ohio was some big deal. It was a serious business. Upon leaving the driveway, Signe found the main roads clear and safe. Snow was still falling in what had to be some record, but the roads services department was equipped to deal with the accumulation.

Retracing her route of the previous evening, Signe found a small strip of stores and filled her economy rental car with food and a few diversions like a small radio and some paperback books. She bought a very good wine and some frozen lasagna Florentine, Kate's favorite. To satiate her starvation, she popped into a very sincere diner named "Yours Truly" and ordered a bowl of vegetable chili and a small focaccia bread.

As she ate it occurred to her how dense she was. Her sister lived in an artists' colony. The women were not in bed, nor had they disappeared. They were in one of the out buildings working. In their politeness, they had not disturbed her. Finishing her meal in haste, she regretted not leaving Kate a note. Her older sister would certain take delight in scolding her.

Returning, the snow again falling with a rapidity well know in this region, Signe wondered if she might become snowed in. Her visit was so short - only two days - she regretted not seeing Kate an entire day. Perhaps she would call the airlines and see about a later flight out so she could maximize her time with her sister.

As the coming weather would unfold, Signe's trip out would be postponed by the hardest storm to hit the Ohio, western New York and Pennsylvania in many a decade. Houses would collapse under the weight. The airport was going to shut down for three days. A record snow of nearly historic proportions would cripple the travel industry. Returning to her sister's house, Kate noted with amazement that the snow, which had already fallen very hard and steady, was actually falling harder. The roads were completely covered. She estimated that perhaps six to eight inches had fallen in the three hours she had gone.

Pulling in the drive, she was surprised to see her sister standing, coatless and worried, under the side door light. Bathed in a cone of yellow, she looked angry and vexed. In fact, her stare was more glare than concern. As she opened the door, grabbing the holders of the numerous blue plastic shopping bags, the house door also opened and the other five women spilled out. Also coatless, they too, held looks of anger and scorn. The usually strong and secure Signe felt a rumbling of uncertainty that she identified as fear.

What followed was an unpleasant confrontation, first with her raging sister, and then, as the others chorused in, between her sister and the house mates. Shouts of "kick her out of here" were balanced by screams of "danger", which Signe assumed meant the snow covered roads. Never once did any of the women look cold or uncomfortable. With an upraised hand, Kate brought the three way altercation to an end and led the way back into the kitchen. Signe, the last one in, was not assisted in bringing in her purchases.

In the kitchen, Signe and Kate were left alone to talk. Signe felt some strangeness from her sister not apparent the previous evening. There was an edge of desperation in her voice as she explained why leaving was not allowed until she left for good. The colony had rules and, since Kate was the first of the group and the house was hers, she had made an exception in letting Signe visit. She confessed that the decision had been wrong and, as soon as the snow let up, she would have to leave.

"Our ways are different from the world's ways," she explained. "We are all but cloistered by choice to concentrate on our creations and work. We allow no visitors and live away from the larger society. Ours is a small circle, completely unlike the world around us. Tomorrow, you must go."

Alone in the kitchen, Signe cried in wonder of what she had done that was so wrong. Leaving her food in the plastic Heinen's bags, she put them away in a cupboard and the refrigerator. Sadly, she returned to her room and closed the door.

Sitting alone she began seeing the strange world she had come to. If an artists' colony, where was the art? The walls were bare of any adornment. The rooms she had seen were sparsely furnishings. Only the kitchen looked lived in.

Hearing noise, she returned to the kitchen to find the six eating again from an enormous common bowl of salsa and chips. Fingers were frequently used as the means to bring food to mouth, but no one cared. Only Kate greeted her with a smile as she ate. The others ignored her entirely. In the midst of the crunching, noisy eating, Signe made herself a cheese sandwich and opened a bottle of iced tea. There was no place to sit so she ate standing.

Kate and the others, whose names she still did not know she suddenly realized, focused all their attention on the rapidly diminishing bowls before them. When the chips were gone, they all scooped the salsa in handfuls and slathered it into their mouths. Two more jars of salsa were opened and poured into the bowl. Signe could not look away at what was becoming an awful horror. No comprehension came to her.

Retiring to the living room, Signe awaited Kate. She attempted to read a book, but could not concentrate. What was she missing? Whatever it was could not penetrate the noisy sounds of eating which seeped from the next room.

Kate came to her after a time and sat next to her on the couch. She looked faint of color and had food on her clothing. Her eyes were sharp, however, and her voice strong as she began a halting apology for how she had behaved. She begged Signe to understand the concern she felt when she found her sister gone in this heavy snow. No explanation was given for her peculiar condemnation of Signe's visit; a visit which Kate had requested and arranged.

The others drifted into the room. They each were as Kate, more relaxed and splattered with bits of tomato and juice. Sleeves were wet with the residue of salsa which Signe imagined had been wiped from their mouths. The immensity of the mysterious way these women behaved and lived descended upon Signe like the mound of snow continuing to fall outside.

As the night wore on, the women became lighter in their mood. Soon they shared stories and laughed. Signe relaxed without realizing it and told stories of Italy. Of great interest were the foods she had discovered in Italy, especially ones, she realized later, which were heavy in tomato or tomato sauce. Signe got her wine and some paper cups she had bought on her shopping trip, and spilled a heavy slosh of the dark red libation into each woman's cup. She drank and toasted and finished her bottle off quickly. When trying to give the others more they politely refuse. She remembered a college phrase that declared in a sing-song voice "*that just means more for me, none for you*"and laughed to herself. A nice buzz was filling her head, relaxing her tongue and attitude.

The night wore on and, once again, the women retired quite late. As she fell into her bed, still fully clothed, she imagined herself looking again out the window at the snow. But somehow she knew it was still piling up.

Her excess drinking and the accumulated exhaustion kept her in bed most of the next day. It was nearly dusk when she rose and left her room searching out some remedy for her lightly throbbing head. In the kitchen the once again eating women did not greet or acknowledge her, but their hateful demeanor toward her was evident.

They would gladly kill me thought Signe as she moved out of the kitchen to the front room.

Unable to consider eating in her nausea, Signe stood in a flash of "been here before" as she considered how identical the scene was to the evening before. Ravenous slurps, foul stares, no concern for civility, the same food. Her awareness spilled over into shock when one of the women went to the pantry to replenish the salsa. There were only a few jars left of the cases she had seen yesterday. The jolt loosened her tongue.

"Kate," Signe began from the kitchen doorway, "can we talk a minute?"

Kate totally ignored her. Signe edged into the room and stood behind her sister.

"Kate. Kate!" she said as she reached out and touched her. Her sister turned on her with fury, reaching for her face and eyes with salsa covered fingers.

"Don't touch me." Kate hissed. She returned to her place at the salsa bowl.

With fear in her blood, Signe edged out of the kitchen and went to her room. She had to pack to catch her plane. Although her flight was twelve hours away, the first of the morning, she needed to occupy herself with activity. After arranging her stuff, she went to the bath room for a shower. The spray came out thick and lightly browned from disuse. She could not bear the dirty water and returned to her room.

Sitting on her bed she felt the bottled up terror she had thus far kept at bay welling up inside in an effort to overwhelm her. Her mind raced over every detail. No art in the art colony. No leaving the property. No visitors. No food, save the salsa. No day life. No phone or TV. And a strange Kate she had never met before, until she transformed late at night when she was her old self after devouring salsa.

Signe tried to pan for nuggets of understanding in the midst of the sands of confusion. Struggling with tears of fear, she edged back to the corner of the bed when Kate entered the room with no knock of announcement. She seemed very serious, although not as agitated as she had seemed in the kitchen. Signe found herself ready to flinch if attacked by her approaching sister.

"You must leave, now, tonight." Kate said. "You have no idea what we are or what we are like. We cannot give you more time with us. You are upsetting our lives and our ways and we need for you to leave. Go and wait at the airport."

All her fears suddenly overwhelmed her and she began to weep. Emitting an involuntary groan, Signe wordlessly scrambled for her back pack and night bag. She needed no begging or explanation. Her intuitions were flashing that she was in danger. Her flight response was ready to launch.

Pulling her bags through the kitchen, she noted that the pantry was open and the salsa entirely gone. This, more than anything, screamed to her of wrongness and some undiscerned evil.

Carrying her coat and offering no goodbye, she ran through the now thigh high snow to the mound that roughly indicated the shape of her car. Revving the engine to get it running smoothly, she used her bare hands to clear the deep snow from her windshield and windows. The six women were standing in the drive ahead of her, a barrier to any possessions she may have forgotten in the house, as if anything she may have left was worth reentering that pit of hell and confusion.

Returning to her place behind the wheel, Signe slowly edged through the deep snow to the road. She spun a half dozen times, but somehow, miraculously, she reached the road. Looking both ways she was startled to find herself greeted by flashing lights from a police car. Blocking her from the main road with his car, a uniformed officer slowly trudged through the drifts to speak with her, tapping on her window. As she rolled the glass down, she noted that the six hags, and that included her sister, were no longer in sight.

"Can't let you on the road, missy," the officer said to her in a patronizing, but refreshingly polite tone. His nametag identified him as Officer C. A. Ramsey. Joining him, his duty partner left the warmth of the police car and stood next to Ramsey. Her nametag pulled rank and Sgt. L Laufik sympathetically and silently assured Signe that she was not going anywhere.

"Storm is too bad and getting badder. We are sending everyone home. Expecting maybe a foot, maybe two more 'fore morning. Best pull back in and hole up till it passes."

"I have to get to the airport." She began groping in her back pack for her ticket to offer as proof. "I'm flying out..." A sinking feeling of knowing filled her as she read his face and interpreted his nodding head.

"Missy, that 'port's boarded up tighter than a church offering box. Nothing coming in and nothing goin' out. Been closed since yesterday and maybe will be for a day or two more. You call 'em. They'll let you know what it's like."

"I have to go." Signe whispered through her thickening throat. The officer simply shook his head no. He watched as she inched back toward the house, making it halfway before the tires spun freely, unconvinced of their need to move the car any further.

Leaving her stuff in the car, Signe ambled back to the house and into the kitchen. The six were there, aware of the reason she had returned. One muttered something about not concerning the law now, after all these years of drawing no attention. Another nodded in agreement. All eyes looked upon her in unmasked hatred tempered only by necessity.

In the kitchen light, Signe noted that the women all looked grayer somehow. There was life in their eyes, but not in their bodies or skin. There was a slumping which went beyond posture. Some new fear was birthed into her guts.

"You have to leave," moaned Kate. "You just have to. I cannot hold out."

The other five retreated to their upstairs rooms, not looking back. Some command had silently passed between them, undetected. In seconds Signe heard the firm closing of doors.

Kate began pacing, flashing glances to her sister. Her repeating course was from table to pantry and back to the table. Her eyes could not comprehend that he salsa cupboard was glaringly and completely empty. They looked over and over again as if looking could produce the jars of mashed tomato and spice.

Signe experienced a fear completely barren of emotion or recognition. Her deepest will to survive was struggling in the face of some unknown, but fully realized enemy.

"What is it, Kate?" she asked quietly.

Seeming to only just remember that her sister was in the room, Kate stopped her pacing and faced Signe, leaving the table as a barrier between her and her sister.

"We are starving. We must eat but we cannot. The weather is keeping us from food. The chickens are gone. Eaten or escaped. We have even eaten all the barn cats and rats. We are dying, and the salsa is gone."

Signe imagined piling logs of fuel on the raging fire of terror in her heart.

Kate began again in a more reasoned tone. "Salsa keeps the hunger down, Signe. Something in its mix of tomatoes, peppers, spices and whatever else makes up salsa gives us a little relief, but it's only temporary and an incomplete substitute. Effective, but without satisfaction."

Her face began contorting in a flash of muscles in conflict. She grabbed her head and pressed in at the temples.

"We need food. Plain and simple. We have to feed. Now."

Signe found her voice through some intervention of all things holy. "Kate, I bought food yesterday. I'll share it. Eat it all, Kate. I'm fine."

"We already looked, Signe. When did you become a blasted vegetarian?"

Suddenly, Kate whipped her face away from Signe. With her head turned she asked again, "When did you quit eating meat, Sigie?"

Stepping around the table, Signe moved to face her sister. From the side she saw a fang as it slowly emerged from Kate's mouth and pressed against her bloodless lips.

"When did you give up meat, Signe? It might have bought you some time. At least a day. Maybe more if it had been some fresh beef full of blood. We only need bits when we run out. Even just what the liner blots up works."

Signe continued to round on her sister, unbelieving what her eyes screamed to her brain was the truth. Only one fang was in place. The other was presumably soon to descend. Rooted to the floor, Signe was a deer in the headlights of her predator sister.

With a scream that likely consisted of every shred of remaining humanity, Kate turned and ran through the door into the night. The force of her lunge knocked the top hinge apart, settling the door open on the porch. The ceaseless snow floated in onto the kitchen floor.

With an explosion of upturned chairs and toppling dishware, the other five burst through the kitchen, ignoring Signe, and dashed through the open, broken door. In the night the sounds of painful howls were dampened and absorbed by the snow covered landscape.

In consuming terror, Kate unthinkingly ran to the feigned security of her room. Later she would remember the policeman and hate herself for not running to him.

Pushing the door closed and shoving the bed against the opposite wall, she crammed her body into the small space between bed and door and held the door shut with her legs and feet. In truth, however, she held no illusion knowing that her efforts would like be futile. If these fanged demons fell upon her, it would be over.

In her hazy panic, Signe dealt with the problem as intellectually as she could. Questions rose about how one becomes as her sister had become. She wondered if she, too, would live as her sister, or if she would only be food.

And as she wondered, in the unstopping continuation of the falling snow, she heard a light tread on the stair outside her door. And a second sound from outside. Like the sound of bone being pulled across glass.

www.ingramcontent.com/pod-product-compliance
Lightning Source LLC
Chambersburg PA
CBHW020844260626
47169CB00003B/1133